Here Lies Jeremy Troy

A Comedy in Three Acts

By Jack Sharkey

A SAMUEL FRENCH ACTING EDITION

SAMUEL FRENCH

FOUNDED 1830

New York Hollywood London Toronto

SAMUELFRENCH.COM

"HERE LIES JEREMY TROY," produced by Elliot Martin, under the direction of Ronny Graham, had its world premiere on August 2, 1965, at the Lakewood Theatre in Skowhegan, Maine, with the following cast:

JEREMY TROY, *a law clerk* .... Will Hutchins
KATHRYN TROY, *his wife* .... Diane Kagan
CHARLIE BICKLE, *an old friend* .... Darren McGavin
TINA WINSLOW, *an undergraduate model* . Ann Willis
SVEN IVORSEN, *Jeremy's boss* .... Murvyn Vye

The time is the present. The action takes place during a twenty-four-hour period in February. The locale of the play is the Troy home in West Rutherford, New Jersey, just a short drive from New York City.

ACT ONE: A weekday morning.

ACT TWO: That evening.

ACT THREE: The following morning.

Critical acclaim for the play was unanimous—

"An applauding success! A smashing hit! The audience roared! A rib tickler if I ever saw one!"

Christiansen/*Bangor Daily News*

"Highly amusing . . . loaded with laughs . . . rapid-fire comical situations . . . steady laughter. During the intermissions, high praise for the new play could be heard everywhere."

Plummer/*Skowhegan Morning Sentinel*

"Even the little old ladies laughed until they wheezed, and I guffawed until my face hurt. This one will get four stars on Broadway, because it can't miss. Funnier than 'Never Too Late,' more laughs than 'Goodbye, Charlie,' and completely involves an audience better than 'The Caine Mutiny.' "

Huntington/*Lewiston Evening Journal*

"A refreshing revelation—clean, sparkling comedy—almost breathless comedy, except the audience needs its breath for the next laugh. Recommended for the whole family. Waves of laughter rolled over the performers on the stage. A five-pointed satellite that promises to sail onto Broadway and shine there for a long time!"

Henderson /*Kennebec Journal*

"Jack Sharkey has a hit on his hands!"

Kup's Column

"The backers of 'Jeremy Troy' will get their money back, year in and out. The show is sure-fire."

Syracuse Herald-Journal

"A hilarious farce, sexy but nice . . . a bright comedy with witty dialogue . . . one just can't help laughing!"

Syracuse Post-Standard

"Jack Sharkey writes better than his namesake could fight!"

Leominster Enterprise (*Massachusetts*)

Here Lies Jeremy Troy

ACT ONE

SCENE: *The Troy home in West Rutherford, New Jersey. The entire Downstage area is the living room, from the large pull-draped picture window with lidded windowseat on the Right wall to the staircase that mounts from Downstage Left to a balcony beginning Upstage left. In the living room are a sofa and coffee table before the window, a desk along the wall masking the underside of the staircase, a telephone, some blue-bound documents and a carved elephant statuette on the desk, and a sturdy hassock just Downstage of the desk. A high-backed chair stands against the wall Downstage of the window. The balcony runs the width of the Upstage wall. Supporting its center is a broad fireplace with mantel, the chimney-section continuing up to the roof on the balcony, but this section is at least three feet farther Upstage than the front of the fireplace itself. On this section hangs a large portrait of George Washington. Just over the mantel hangs a sedate pastoral scene. The two arches formed by balcony, fireplace and Left and Right walls lead to a passageway along the Upstage wall beneath the balcony; at the Right end of this passageway is the visible doorway to the kitchen; at the Left end is the unseen front door to the house. Also unseen, behind the fireplace, is an area where hats and coats can be hung, and—in the Upstage wall—the door to the cellar. Three doors give onto the balcony: at the extreme Right end, directly over the kitchen doorway, is the door to the*

5

bathroom; symmetrically flanking the chimney sec-
tion are the door to the bedroom, Left, and the door
to the guest room, Right. The time is early morning
in the midst of a very cold February. The drapes of
the window are open and the room is bright. As the
Scene begins, KATHRYN TROY *is Onstage but unseen,*
on her hands and knees behind and Upstage of the
sofa. A moment after Curtain-rise, JEREMY TROY
enters from the bathroom and moves toward the bed-
room, in a white shirt, tying his necktie. He is
trouserless. JEREMY *is in his early thirties, and of*
attractive aspect. KATHRYN, *in her late twenties, will*
be—when we see her—as prettily feminine as he is
handsomely male.

JEREMY. (*Agitated.*) Honey, did you find them yet?

KATHRYN. (*Straightens from behind sofa, on knees.*)
Not yet, Jeremy. Are you sure you had them on last
night?

JEREMY. Of course I'm sure. I remember quite clearly.

KATHRYN. Then I wish you'd remember quite clearly
where you took them off.

JEREMY. I was too tired to notice. Have you tried over
by the desk? That's where I spent *most* of last night,
after all. (*Exits into bedroom.*)

KATHRYN. (*Stands, hurries to the desk, searches,*
stands irresolute, then:) They're not here—

JEREMY. (*Comes out, adjusting tie-tack.*) They've got
to be. I can't show up at the office without them, today
of all days! You know how Mr. Ivorsen feels about em-
ployees who don't appreciate his generosity. (*Vanishes*
again into bedroom.)

KATHRYN. Well then, why couldn't he have given you
an *extra* set·of cuff links for Christmas? (*Finds empty*
tumbler on mantel, looks at it, gets an idea, carries it off
with her into kitchen.)

JEREMY. (*Enters, now in trousers, suit jacket over arm*
and briefcase in hand, starts downstairs.) Did you try in

the—? (*Stops speaking as* KATHRYN *re-enters with ice cube tray, sets his briefcase on desk, meets her before the fireplace.*)

KATHRYN. (*Lifts out divider on:*) They were in the ice cube tray. (*As he takes them, starts inserting them into cuffs.*) You didn't tell me you had a highball last night.

JEREMY. (*Business of getting helped into suit jacket.*) I thought you would have guessed. It's no fun working all night unless I can promise myself a reward when I'm done. But there it is! (*Lifts documents on desk, flourishes and replaces them during:*) The result of three back-breaking weeks of correlating case histories, judicial decisions, regulations, by-laws and loopholes into one of the tightest defénses the firm of Ivorsen and Motz has ever possessed. And I am beat.

KATHRYN. (*Has gotten his overcoat behind fireplace, helps him into it on:*) Poor darling! Listen—why don't you take the day off? You've certainly earned it. I can take your brief into New York for you. It's not far.

JEREMY. (*Tempted, hesitates, then shakes his head.*) Nope. If it were any day but today, I might do it. But I can't very well call in sick, and then be a charming host when Mr. Ivorsen comes for dinner tonight.

KATHRYN. (*Buttoning overcoat, adjusting lapels, etc.*) Do you think it'll happen, darling? Are you sure? I mean, Mr. Motz has only been dead for two months—

JEREMY. After Mr. Ivorsen sees that brief, I'll be a shoo-in for the full partnership. (*Dreaming aloud.*) "Ivorsen and Troy"! Has a nice ring, doesn't it?

KATHRYN. (*Fondly.*) It's no more than you deserve, Jeremy. After all—seven years with the firm. Seven long, hard years.

JEREMY. (*Takes her by the shoulders to face him.*) Seven *wonderful* years. What man couldn't be a success with a woman like you at his side?

KATHRYN. (*Dryly.*) A steeplejack.

JEREMY. (*Laughs, gives her a quick peck on the lips.*) Now if you'll excuse me, I've got to run. I called a cab from upstairs, and it'll be here any minute. (*Stoops and pulls a metal strongbox from the bottom drawer of desk.*) Listen, I think my diploma's in here someplace. Will you see if you can find it and tack it up where old Ivorsen will be sure to see it? Just in case he hasn't mentioned my promotion by the time I come home tonight. Every little nudge helps. (*Sets box on Upstage front corner of desk.*)

KATHRYN. (*Gestures kitchenward.*) Are you sure you don't want to take the car, dear?

JEREMY. You'll need it more than I do, what with all the high-priced food you're going to have to get today. We want Ivorsen— (*HORN honks Offstage Left.*) feeling jolly, remember!

KATHRYN. Your cab's here—you'd better run, darling—

JEREMY. (*Grabs briefcase from desk.*) Listen, I'll phone if I get the promotion down at the office. But if he doesn't mention it, well— You'd better be at your absolute most charming tonight, then— (*Pecks her on lips.*) and make the martinis five-to-one! (*Starts for front door.*)

KATHRYN. (*Points at his feet.*) Your galoshes! The weatherman said snow!

JEREMY. No time, darling. I really have to run. (*Steps from sight toward front door, then rushes back to her.*) Good luck. To *both* of us! (*Kisses her once more; HORN honks again; toward cab:*) Okay-okay! (*Exits with a SLAM of front door.*)

KATHRYN. (*Sighs with relief at completion of the daily off-to-work ritual, starts to pick up strongbox, sees what we have seen all along: the brief still sits on the desk; grabs it up.*) Oh, no! Jeremy! (*Even as she runs with it toward door, we hear ENGINE start as the cab pulls away; she hurries back to desk, drops brief on desk, lifts phone, dials, and:*) Hello? . . . This is Mrs. Jeremy Troy, at five-thirty-one Pinecrest Drive. One of your cabs just picked up my husband and he's forgotten some very important papers—to New York . . . You will? . . . Oh, thank you. Thank you so very much! (*Hangs up, starts to bring ice cube tray back toward kitchen; door CHIMES sound.*) Well, *that* was quick! (*Goes to front door, opens it, and we hear:*)

CHARLIE. (*Starts line off, but enters during first few words.*) Hello, hello, hello! My name is Charlie Bickle. I know the name may mean nothing to you now, but someday the whole world will know it. (CHARLIE *is dressed in slacks, sweater and open-necked shirt. He carries a duffel bag, a framed canvas, folded easel, and box of brushes and paints, all of which he drops Upstage of sofa during his swift-striding entrance, and his continuing speech is emphasized by a rapt outfling of his arms, Right, on:*) Great godfrey! That window! And a north light, too! That's what every artist dreams of, a north light—I forget exactly why.

KATHRYN. (*Following him in more slowly, a bit breathtaken.*) Bickle . . . Charlie Bickle— Are you a friend of Jeremy's?

CHARLIE. (*Has turned to her, points to her on:*) Please! Don't speak! Just stand there and let me drink in your beauty. Better yet, let me drink in your wine cellar, if you have one. Say you have a wine cellar—

KATHRYN. (*Still dazed, but becoming amused.*) But we haven't—

CHARLIE. You are *not* following *instructions* . . . But where's old Jer?

KATHRYN. You just missed him, but you're in luck. He forgot some important papers, so I called the cab company. They have radiophones or something. He should be back at any moment— You know, you're not dressed very warmly for this weather? Can I get you a cup of coffee?

CHARLIE. I make it a practice never to drink coffee on an empty stomach. You see, I have this old football injury— (*Strikes classic pigskin-hurling stance.*)

KATHRYN. (*Places him.*) Charlie Bickle—from the university! No wonder your name was familiar! Why, you were the star quarterback for four years—

CHARLIE. *You* went to the university? How did I ever miss *meeting* you?

KATHRYN. Oh, I didn't attend the school. I lived in town, but I used to go up to the campus for all the social activities. That's how I met Jeremy. At one of the dances. He'll be awfully pleased to see you after all these years. Do you know, you're the first school friend we've seen since Jeremy's graduation?

CHARLIE. (*Who's been casing the place during her speech.*) This room—it's magnificent! I can't tell you what I'd give just to own those ten square feet of carpet in front of that window! . . . Did I tell you I'm a painter?

KATHRYN. Not in so many words. But you drop your clues very deftly.

CHARLIE. (*A bit of sincerity pokes through the brusque facade.*) Was I as bad as all that, Mrs. Troy?

KATHRYN. "Kathryn," please! Not bad, Charlie. Just —overwhelming . . . Oh, but I'm forgetting your empty stomach. (*Starts for kitchen.*) What kind of football injury did you have, anyway?

CHARLIE. (*Calls, as she exits:*) An ulcer! I had this deepseated anxiety against getting tackled. It hurts. I was the only player on the team who used to scream during scrimmage. For me the water boy carried crackers and milk.

KATHRYN. (*Enters with hastily assembled tray of coffeecake, coffeepot, etc.*) But you were the fastest quarterback the university ever had. (*Sets tray on coffee table, sits on sofa, pours for them, during:*) When you took that ball down the field you never let an opposing player anywhere near you.

CHARLIE. (*Munching, sipping, etc.*) Now you know why: I was terrified!

KATHRYN. (*Laughs; then:*) But tell me, Charlie, what brings you to this part of the country?

CHARLIE. A bus. From the Port Authority Terminal. I've lived in New York for years, now. You know: Greenwich Village, sidewalk shows, bongo drums, espresso coffee— I even had a beard for awhile, but people kept mistaking me for Commander Whitehead, so I gave it up. The only "jolly little Bubbles" *I* knew was this exotic dancer who— Hmm, I guess I should know you a bit better before telling you *that* story . . . (*Paces restlessly as he munches, drinking in the fascination of the picture window, a bundle of exuberant energy.*)

KATHRYN. But if you live so close by, why haven't you dropped in before?

CHARLIE. Oh—you know how it is: One of those things you keep *meaning* to do, but never get around to—like writing your congressman. (*Eager to change the subject from this patent evasion:*) Say, where's your bathroom? My fingers are a little sticky from your generosity . . . (*Starts upstairs without waiting for:*)

KATHRYN. Right up there—

CHARLIE. (*At bedroom.*) In here?

KATHRYN. No, that's our bedroom—

CHARLIE. (*At guest room.*) In here?

KATHRYN. No, that's the guest room—

CHARLIE. Guest room! (*Kisses his hand, slaps kiss on door, then:*) In *here!* (*Exits into bathroom on:*)

KATHRYN. Yes! (*Slumps back in place on sofa, recovering from this whirlwind, and then front door SLAMS.*) Is that you, dear?

JEREMY. (*Enters, busily starts stuffing brief into case, on:*) No, it's *me!*

KATHRYN. (*Rises, starts for him, a woman with a surprise; gets hinty:*) You have a visitor, Jeremy. An old friend.

JEREMY. (*Still busy fastening case, etc.*) Male or female?

KATHRYN. His name is Charlie. Does that help?

JEREMY. (*Finishing up.*) The world is full of Charlies, darling. Which one is this, and where is he? I really have to dash—

(*Upstairs,* CHARLIE *comes from bathroom, sees* JEREMY,
and starts fast, on tiptoe, for stairs, during:)

KATHRYN. (*Sotto voce:*) He's up in the bathroom.

JEREMY. Look, will you tell him I couldn't wait? If he
wanted to see me, why'd he go to the bathroom?

KATHRYN. I guess *he* couldn't wait, either. Well, don't
worry, I'll make your excuses, Jeremy. You'd better scoot.

JEREMY. (*Back toward stairs, doesn't see* CHARLIE *descending.*) Okay. I'm *really* in a rush, now. Would've
been back sooner, but we got stuck in the middle lane of
tunnel traffic, and couldn't turn around till Union City—

CHARLIE. (*From vantage point a few stairs up, flings
out arms.*) Jeremy-boy!

JEREMY. (*Turns, sees him.*) Charlie . . . Charlie Bickle
—from the *university!* (*Falls backward in dead faint
onto floor.*)

KATHRYN. Jeremy!

CHARLIE. (*Beat; lowers his arms; then:*) Well—he
remembers me, all right!

(*He and* KATHRYN *now hurry to* JEREMY, *loosening his
coat, etc.*)

KATHRYN. I was afraid this would happen. Drive, drive,
drive, day and night, and *now* look!

JEREMY. (*Seated on floor between them, wakes facing*
KATHRYN.) What happened? What time is it? (*Turns
head, sees* CHARLIE.) Oh. It *is* you, Charlie! (*Faints
again.*)

CHARLIE. (*To a still-stunned* KATHRYN.) You know
. . . I'm honored. This is the first time in my life anybody was so glad to see me that he passed out cold. (*As*
JEREMY *starts reviving again, helps him to his feet,
during:*) Here, you'd better sit down, Jer. You don't
look so good.

JEREMY. (*Wobbly, getting onto sofa.*) I don't feel so
good, either.

KATHRYN. (*Anger overriding concern.*) Then that settles it. You're taking the day off, and I'm taking that brief into New York for you.

JEREMY. Kathy— Would you? (*Rises, voice grateful, but manner urgent; is practically pushing here into her coat and out of the house, on:*) I sure do appreciate it, darling. You're a wife in a million—

KATHRYN. What'll I tell Mr. Ivorsen about tonight? Is dinner on or off?

JEREMY. *On*, of course! Now hurry. Tell Ivorsen I'll try to get in to the office this afternoon. (*Shoves her out of sight toward front door, turns, starts toward* CHARLIE *with index finger pointing, as if about to rage, when:*)

KATHRYN. (*Re-enters, arms akimbo.*) The BRIEF!

JEREMY. (*Grabs case from desk so fast it sends strong-box flying onto floor, disgorging contents all over: papers, photos, etc.*) Here! Now hurry, darling—the meter's running!

KATHRYN. Jeremy, if you're sick—

JEREMY. All I need is a short nap and I'll be good as new. Now, please *scram*, dear! (*Pushes her out again, and we hear front door SLAM;* CHARLIE *begins picking up papers from floor;* JEREMY *re-enters, sees him.*) What do you think you're *doing*?

CHARLIE. Just cleaning up after the hurricane, old buddy—

JEREMY. Well, stop it. I mean— You're my guest, Charlie. It's not your place to do the housework for me—

CHARLIE. Say, are you all right, Jer? Maybe you *should* take that nap—

JEREMY. I'm perfectly fine. Now, just give me those.

CHARLIE. (*About to hand papers over, pauses to look at one.*) Gee, *I* didn't know you made summa cum laude.

JEREMY. My diploma! What are you doing with it?

CHARLIE. (*Increasingly uneasy in the presence of his maniacal host.*) Just reading it, is all. And admiring it. I think what you did takes a lot of courage. Your wife sure admires you.

JEREMY. Good grief, you didn't tell *Kathryn* what I did, did you? She loves me, trusts me, admires me—

CHARLIE. And why shouldn't she? Any guy who works his way through college the way you did— What do you mean, "tell her"? She already knows. Doesn't she?

JEREMY. (*Frozen, with semi-hysterical grin:*) Of *course* she knows . . . I was only *joking*.

CHARLIE. (*Now eager to be gone.*) Uh—look, old buddy—maybe I better be on my way and you can take that nap like you were supposed to, huh—?

JEREMY. (*Still in overcoat, hat, lies back on sofa, head toward window and hands folded on stomach over bulk of strongbox.*) Yes!—yes, do that—so I can nap! Nice seeing you again! You'd better hurry. There may be snow.

CHARLIE. (*Backing into archway.*) Don't get up. (*Steps from sight;* JEREMY *bounds to his feet, rushes to desk, sets down strongbox, starts to dial phone.* CHARLIE *re-enters behind him, as if about to speak to him on sofa, sees him at phone, reacts, then says uncomfortably:*) There's just one thing, Jeremy— (JEREMY *stiffens, shuts eyes briefly, hangs up phone, waits.*) the *real* reason I came by, today.·

JEREMY. (*Thinks "it has happened" at last; sighs resignedly, echoes:*) The real reason. All right. How much do you want, Charlie?

CHARLIE. (*Hurt, angry.*) Aww . . . You've been talking to Henry Schmidlapp!

JEREMY. (*Blankly.*) I have?

CHARLIE. Whose word are you going to take, his or mine?

JEREMY. About *what*, Charlie?

CHARLIE. Oh, stop trying to spare my feelings, Jer. Henry *must've* told you about me. Just because I over-extended my stay at his apartment in 1962!

JEREMY. How long did you stay?

CHARLIE. Till 1964 . . . See, Jer, the way I figure, an artist doesn't need much in life except a place to work. And what with the alumni numbering in the thousands, it's only natural that a good percentage of them live in or near New York City, so—

JEREMY. You've been leeching off the alumni!

CHARLIE. (*Proudly impartial:*) In alphabetical order. Now I'm up to the *T*'s. Take your turn like a man.

JEREMY. But—where were you between Schmidlapp and Troy?

CHARLIE. (*Ticks them off on his fingers:*) With, uh—Sheridan . . . Sherman . . . Slaughter . . . Sloane . . . Smith . . . Smith . . . Smith . . . uh . . . *Smith!* . . . Stokey . . . Thompson— And then I sold a painting for five hundred bucks and got my own place in the Village.

JEREMY. Then what are you doing *here?*

CHARLIE. Oh, I frittered away the five hundred on frivolities like food, rent, gas, electricity, water—

JEREMY. (*Overjoyed with relief.*) Well, why didn't you *say* so? Here, take a hundred bucks, old pal— (*Fumbles bills out of wallet.*)

CHARLIE. Oh, no, Jer, I couldn't—really, that's too much! I— (*Grabs money and pockets it swiftly on:*) Twenty bucks would've been fine! (*As* JEREMY *puts wallet back in pocket, starts to pick up last of papers from floor.*)

JEREMY. Here, now, *I'll* do that—

CHARLIE. Hell, for a hundred bucks it's the least I can— (*Stops, looking at photograph.*) Gee, it's funny how all these old graduation pictures look alike! Everybody on the steps of the administration building in their caps and gowns. You can't tell 'em apart from one year to the next. Why, a guy couldn't tell this group from the one in *my* old graduation picture. I remember I was standing right over— (*Runs finger along photograph, stops.*) Hey. That's me. How'd you get hold of *my* graduation picture, Jer? (JEREMY *just stands mute, frozen with fear.*) It's the damnedest thing . . . I never paid much attention before, but there's a guy right behind me, at the end of the back row, who looks just like *you* . . . What'd they do, chum, stick you with the wrong picture?

JEREMY. (*Faintly.*) Wr-wrong picture?

CHARLIE. Well, sure! I mean, this picture is the wrong year.

JEREMY. (*Sickly echo:*) Wrong year.

CHARLIE. (*Takes diploma from papers at desk.*) Hell, just look at the date on your diploma: "Class of—" (*Beat.*) Hey, that's the same year *I* graduated. But that's impossible. I mean, I know for a fact that while *I* was finishing up my senior year, you hadn't even *begun* the college yet. You were still saving for your tuition, working as— (*It starts to hit him.*) as the file clerk— (*It's almost upon him.*) in the *reg-is-trar's of-fice.* . . ! (*Wheels slowly to read the truth in* JEREMY'S *stricken grin.*)

JEREMY. Uh. Funny. How they could make *two* errors. Picture *and* diploma.

CHARLIE. (*Stunned.*) Jeremy—you never *did* go to law school! You never got a degree at *all!*

JEREMY. (*Grasping at straws.*) Does this look like the home of a man without a college education?

CHARLIE. Does this look like the graduation picture of a man in law school? This is the Liberal Arts Class!

JEREMY. Charlie—I can explain—

CHARLIE. Well, I should certainly *hope* so! How the hell did you manage to get where you are today on a phony diploma? (*Sits on sofa, dazed by developments.*)

JEREMY. (*Not quite wringing his hands, but almost, remains standing, for:*) Wellll— It was just—one of those things. One day I was a clerk in the registrar's office and the next thing I knew I was up for a full partnership in a big law firm.

CHARLIE. Sure. Just like that. Happens every day.

JEREMY. (*Slightly more relaxed, tries to delve into circumstances himself, as if never having really thought it through until now.*) Actually—I guess you might say it all began with Kathryn. In a way, even, you might say it was all her fault—

CHARLIE. Aw, come off it, Jer! Just how did *Kathryn* start you on your life of sin?

JEREMY. She said she loved me.

CHARLIE. That'll *do* it!

JEREMY. (*Suddenly eager to confess, as if a pent-up inner dam had burst, sits down half-turned to face* CHARLIE *on sofa, appealing to him.*) You've got to understand, Charlie! Here I was—a nothing, a nobody—working all day, just filing, filing, filing at a big university. Thousands of new students each year. Files, grades, classes, courses of study—*you* know. Then one night, at a dance, I meet Kathryn. She's young, she's beautiful, and she *likes* me. We get to talking. She tells me if there's one thing she's nuts about, it's men who use their brains, men who don't squander their time away fussing at menial work, men who aspire to higher things—

CHARLIE. In short, she loves everything you ain't—

JEREMY. Exactly. So instead of correcting her assumption that I'm a student, I say nothing. It's too late to tell her I'm just a simple clerk.

CHARLIE. Nothing simple about the way *you* clerked!

JEREMY. Well. Be that as it may. She finally asked me which school I was attending. I said law. I don't know why. It was the first thing popped into my head, law.

CHARLIE. Probably because you were breaking it—

JEREMY. Anyhow, she told me she was just wild about lawyers. That's when I decided that's what I'd have to become. So the next day, when nobody was in the office, I got at the files, filled out a registration card for the five previous years in my name. I made up classes, courses, attendance records, marks—

CHARLIE. *Good* marks, too. It's not everyone graduates summa cum laude.

JEREMY. Well. You know. If you're gonna tell a lie, make it a good one. Besides, Kathryn was looking forward to attending my graduation. I didn't want to be at the bottom of the class.

CHARLIE. No, 1 guess not. What rank *were* you?

JEREMY. First.

CHARLIE. (*Lurches to his feet, aghast.*) *First?*

JEREMY. (*Reminiscence has his face aglow with joy, now.*) Yeah, I took top honors. You should've heard the applause when I ascended to the podium for my diploma. The governor was there. He shook my hand.

CHARLIE. (*Pacing distractedly.*) But that's crazy! How could you get away with it? How could you even have *hoped* to get away with it?

JEREMY. (*Stops him, speaks in an almost fatherly manner.*) Charlie, you don't understand big—really big—universities: Nobody knows your name. You're only a little card with a lot of grades on it. Even the teachers don't know who's who. Why, the head of the law department congratulated me, said he'd been keeping his eye on me and knew I had it in me all along!

CHARLIE. (*Mind reeling, gamely stays on his feet.*) But—how'd you end up in the Liberal Arts Class picture, then?

JEREMY. Well, like you said before, all those class pictures look alike. So I just rented a cap and gown and joined the first group I could find posing . . . It's a damn nice picture . . . (*Looks at it wistfully, puts it back on desk.*)

CHARLIE. (*Still struggling to surface from under this flood of revelation.*) But how'd you get into this law firm? You couldn't pass the bar exam—

JEREMY. Never had to take it. Mostly, I only do what I used to do back in the registrar's office: I file things.

CHARLIE. But you don't know anything about *law*—

JEREMY. Filing is filing. All you really need to know is the alphabet.

CHARLIE. But the technical things—what if somebody asks you a legal question?

JEREMY. I answer it. Like the other day, Mr. Ivorsen said to me, "Jeremy, I'm preparing a speech for next month's convention in Philadelphia. What's a good example of a really rough property settlement case?"

CHARLIE. And you said—?

JEREMY. "Johnson versus Weems, Appellate Court of Denver, Colorado, April the 18th, 1934!" He thanked me and wrote it into his speech.

CHARLIE. But what if he looks it up?

JEREMY. Nobody *ever* looks it up. The important thing about being a lawyer is to *sound* as if you're right.

CHARLIE. You are smack out of your mind! *How* long do you think you can keep this kind of thing *up?*

JEREMY. Forever, far as I can see. After all these years, it's become a way of life. Besides, what possible *harm* am I doing?

CHARLIE. (*Looking on the bright side.*) Not as much as if Kathryn had been wild about *brain surgeons!* (*Imagines consequences of that, winces visibly.*)

JEREMY. Kathryn must never learn the truth. It would ruin everything.

CHARLIE. (*Trying to plead his friend back to sanity.*) But she's *bound* to find out, *some* day. She almost did today. Why, if I'd said the wrong thing— "Ruin everything"?

JEREMY. If the truth came out, I'd lose my job, this house, the furniture. Everything's been bought on credit and credit cards. (*Slumps unhappily on sofa, facing Downstage.*) Charlie, don't you realize what keeping my secret *means?*

CHARLIE. (*While visions of sugarplums, etc.*) Yeah. Yeah! (*On* JEREMY'S *next speech, rubs hands together gleefully, takes painting down from over mantel, sticks it out of sight in kitchen, takes impressionistic horror of his own from gear behind sofa, hangs it in other picture's stead.*)

JEREMY. (*Brooding aloud, pays no attention to* CHARLIE.) Oh, I've wanted to tell her the truth, so many times. I plan to do it as a surprise, every anniversary. But I always lose my nerve. (CHARLIE, *meanwhile, goes to desk, rummages in drawers, finds phone book, starts searching through yellow pages.*) In effect, I'd be telling her that all these years she's been living with a stranger.

CHARLIE. (*Still searching, with extra meaning:*) What's so tough about living with a stranger?

JEREMY. She might take it terribly hard. She might even leave me.

CHARLIE. (*Finds number, pulls phone to him, rattles off emotionlessly:*) Jeremy-don't-be-silly-Kathryn-would-never-leave-you-she-loves-you! (*Starts to dial.*)

JEREMY. (*Bemused, starts back slowly toward him, thinking aloud:*) If I lost Kathryn, nothing else would matter. What good is all this nice suburban living, alone?

CHARLIE. Jeremy, if I were you, I would never worry about being alone again. (*Finishes dialing, waits, and to fill hiatus says:*) What would *your* reaction be if *Kathryn* had a deep, dark past? Would you turn on her—throw her out—stop loving her?

JEREMY. Of course not! I'm crazy about her—

CHARLIE. Yet by your ówn admission— (*Listens at phone, hangs up.*) Busy. Yet by your own admission, you're a sneak and a liar. If *you* can be loyal, why not credit *her* with as much loyalty? (*Re-dials.*)

JEREMY. No. I won't tell her. After all, your showing up here today was a chance in a million.

CHARLIE. You're telling me! A chance like this comes once in a lifetime. (*Hangs up.*) Still busy.

JEREMY. And even if she did forgive me, even if she stayed with me—how long could she go on loving a husband who was living a lie at the office every day? (*Sees painting over fireplace, gazes at it appraisingly.*)

CHARLIE. What lie? Once she knows, she could help you go through night school and *get* a degree. You could become what you claim to be.

JEREMY. Why are we even discussing it? Once you've gone, things will be right back to normal again, with the odds against discovery increased in my favor . . . (*The presence of the painting registers; asks, curious and pleased:*) Hey, what's that for?

CHARLIE. Try to think of it as your reward for the wonderful windfall you dropped in my lap.

JEREMY. Aw, you didn't have to do that. What's a hundred dollars?

CHARLIE. (*Dialing again.*) I didn't mean the hundred dollars. Some gifts are more precious than gold.

JEREMY. (*Uneasy, but uncertain why.*) Name two.

CHARLIE. I was referring to your confidence in my discretion. Imagine—the one person in the world who knows your secret is little old me! (*Points at his gear Upstage of sofa.*) Say, would you mind putting that stuff up in the guest room? (JEREMY *starts to, automatically, then stops, stunned, during:*) Hel-lo! Is this the Left Bank Modeling Academy?

JEREMY. (*Turns, reeling, gaping and horrified.*) Now, Charlie—uh—let's discuss this thing calmly—

CHARLIE. I'd like to rent one of your girls for the day—

JEREMY. Look—we're both men of the world—

CHARLIE. Oh, that's too bad . . . Isn't there anybody—? . . . Who?—

JEREMY. Listen, this has gone far enough—

CHARLIE. What did you say her name was?

JEREMY. It's invasion of privacy—

CHARLIE. Why, she should be perfect—

JEREMY. Criminal extortion!

CHARLIE. I'm at five-thirty-one—uh—?

JEREMY. (*As* CHARLIE *looks at him, responds out of reflex:*) Pinecrest Drive. (*Shuts eyes, smacks forehead with palm at own stupidity.*)

CHARLIE. —Pinecrest Drive!

JEREMY. An outrage against all common decency—

CHARLIE. It's the Jeremy Troy residence—the name's on the bell.

JEREMY. (*Realizes—and is furious at—the double insult:*) Charlie Bickle, you're not *listening* to me!

CHARLIE. Swell! (*Hangs up, rubs hands, starts toward gear.*) They're sending me a Miss Winslow. She's only an undergraduate but she needs the experience for her thesis. (*Grabs duffel bag, starts for stairs.*) You'll like her. *She* hasn't got a diploma yet, *either*—

JEREMY. There are *laws* against this sort of thing—

CHARLIE. (*Stops on first stair, turns.*) Are you sure?

JEREMY. (*Goes to speak, then slumps.*) No.

CHARLIE. (*Relieved, trots cheerily upstairs, on:*) Since she's an undergraduate, it'll only cost five dollars an hour. Which—thanks to your generous donation—leaves me financially set for the next twenty hours!

JEREMY. (*Remains downstairs, dazed, almost babbling with apprehension.*) Charlie— You're not going to paint her in *here?*

CHARLIE. Well, I *could* use your front lawn . . . but that'd be kind of chilly for the model. (*At guest room door.*) And now, if you'll excuse me, I'm going to take a shower and get into my working clothes. (*Exits into guest room.*)

JEREMY. (*Fear-paralyzed, moves upstairs at last, zombie-like, wild-eyed.*) Charlie—if it were any other night—but my entire career—everything I've worked for all these years—it all hinges on the outcome of dinner tonight—my boss is coming—things are gonna be tense enough—

CHARLIE. (*Emerges from guest room, minus duffel bag and bare from waist up, en route to bathroom, as* JEREMY *reaches head of stairs.*) And you're afraid of what might happen if he meets me? Well, I wouldn't put you in a spot like that—

JEREMY. (*Lurches toward him, hopefully.*) You mean you're *going?*

CHARLIE. (*Holds* JEREMY *off with hand to chest at bathroom doorway.*) No. But I promise not to sell him a painting— (JEREMY *groans, turns, lurches back toward bedroom.*) Was it something I said?

JEREMY. I need a tranquillizer—I need a *lot* of tranquillizers! (*Reels into bedroom.*)

CHARLIE. Say, would you mind getting the door when

Miss Winslow arrives? (*We hear an incoherent scream from* JEREMY *in bedroom;* CHARLIE *shrugs, as if puzzled by his host's behavior, exits into bathroom;* JEREMY *re-emerges from bedroom, has to support himself on stair railing as he starts downstairs, clutching tranquillizer bottle; when he's halfway down,* CHARLIE *pops head out of bathroom.*) By the way, Kathryn makes great coffee. Pour me a cup, will you? With the late hours we artis's keep, I'm gonna need all the caffeine I can get. (CHARLIE *pops in again;* JEREMY, *mouth working soundlessly, raises his fist to shake it at bathroom door before speaking, then stops as he sees the bottle the hand holds; he looks more closely at it, then over at coffee pot on coffee table; slowly, and almost stealthily, he makes his way over to the pot, looks at it and at the bottle again, then back up over shoulder at bathroom, and back to bottle; as though frightened at his own deed, pulls the cap from the bottle, then reaches for the lid of coffee pot, then straightens, fists clenched to chest, eyes shut, and shakes his head; he is about to replace cap when* CHARLIE *pops head out of bathroom again.*) Hey, Jer—?

JEREMY. (*Jumps guiltily, keeps bottle tight to chest, does not turn head to face* CHARLIE.) What?

CHARLIE. I hope your boss likes chicken cacciatore.

JEREMY. Why?

CHARLIE. 'Cause that's what I've decided we're having.

(CHARLIE *pops out again, shuts bathroom door;* JEREMY'S *face is a study in fury at this last straw; swiftly, without any more hesitation, whips lid from pot, dumps contents of bottle into it, slams lid back on, swirls pot to dissolve pills, during:*)

JEREMY. Oh, Char-leee! . . . I'm putting the coffee and stuff on the tab-le! . . . I guess you've got me over a barrel, all right . . . Make yourself— (*Starts for desk, drops bottle in drawer, finds listing in open phonebook, starts to dial rapidly.*) at home, old buddy—drink *all* the

coffee you want! (*Lowers voice to urgent whisper, on:*)
Hello? Is this the Left Bank? . . . Well, this is Jeremy
Troy. One of your models was supposed to come over
here, but the artist contracted an unexpected case of sleeping sickness, and— What? . . . *When?* . . . Oh, okay,
thanks, I'll head her off at the bus stop! (*Slams down
phone, bolts for kitchen doorway, but stops in archway
as we hear front DOOR slam.*)

KATHRYN. (*Off.*) Honey? (*Enters Left, anxiously, removing coat.*) Honey, I'm home—

JEREMY. (*Looks in bewilderment at watch, whirls to
face her.*) You *can't* be!

KATHRYN. I was so worried about you, I decided to
send the brief with the cab driver, and took another cab
back here. You looked so ghastly when I left—

JEREMY. Well. Um. I'm fine, now. I—uh—I suppose
you'll be starting dinner pretty soon, huh?

KATHRYN. At ten o'clock in the morning? I haven't
even done my shopping—

JEREMY. I mean—what with peeling potatoes and all—

KATHRYN. I'm using instant mashed. With enough
butter and milk, he'll never know the difference! (*Has
left coat over back of desk chair, purse on desk, and is
moving toward him when her gaze falls on the painting.*)
Jeremy, what in the world is *that?*

JEREMY. Uh. A sort of gift from Charlie.

KATHRYN. Charlie—? Good heavens, I'd forgotten all
about him—

JEREMY. *How?*

KATHRYN. (*Another step toward him, sees gear still behind sofa.*) His things—? I don't— Jeremy! You *didn't*
ask him to *stay?*

JEREMY. Uh. Not exactly . . . (*His mind is working
furiously; he moves toward desk.*)

KATHRYN. But he *can't* stay—not tonight! I have
everything planned—you'll have to tell him *no.*

JEREMY. *Charlie?*

KATHYRN. Well, he can't *stay*—

JEREMY. But he's *got* to stay—
KATHRYN. Why?
JEREMY. There's a reason—
KATHRYN. What reason?
JEREMY. A good reason—
KATHRYN. I hope it *is*—
JEREMY. Oh, it is—
KATHRYN. Well, what is it?
JEREMY. (*He has been stalling for time; now his eye lights upon the carved elephant on the desk; he grabs it up, thinks fast, then turns to face her, solemnly, holding it at chest height.*) Kathryn. You remember the legend about the elephant's graveyard?
KATHRYN. You mean like in that Tarzan movie? Yes—
JEREMY. Well—it's the same thing with Charlie—
KATHRYN. He's searching for ivory?
JEREMY. No, no! You know how in the legend, when an elephant knows it's going to die, it seeks out a certain spot in the jungle and goes there to spend its last hours on earth? Well, Charlie has decided that this is the place for him. He wants to stay here.
KATHRYN. (*As if completing his line:*) Till the elephants show up. (*Starts for him.*) Jeremy, you're not well!
JEREMY. I'm perfectly fine, I assure you—
KATHRYN. But there hasn't been an elephant in this part of New Jersey since— (*Realizes she's speaking like an idiot, stops; goes for stairs.*) I'm going to take your temperature—
JEREMY. (*Remains by desk as she passes, shouts desperately:*) Darling, you don't understand! Charlie has come here to *die!*

(*She takes one more step, then it sinks in; she turns, wide-eyed; he solemnly hands elephant to her.*)

KATHRYN. (*Holds it between palms, looks down at it; beat; then:*) But— Mr. Ivorsen's coming— And— Charlie looked so healthy!

JEREMY. Darling, Charlie may *look* hale and hearty, but deep down inside—

KATHRYN. His ulcer!

JEREMY. Ulcer?

KATHRYN. (*Absently stroking elephant's back, as if it were the man himself.*) Oh, the poor man . . . I had no idea his ulcer was so serious . . . (*Suddenly regains her level-headedness.*) Now, wait a minute—he can't have an ulcer! Jeremy, that man *eats* like an elephant— (*Thumps statuette back onto desk with finality.*)

JEREMY. (*Improvising desperately.*) It—it doesn't act up *all* the time, darling . . . only if you mention the university—

KATHRYN. The football part!

JEREMY. *Any* part! So whatever you do, don't let Charlie talk about the university. It could be fatal—

KATHRYN. How do I stop him?

JEREMY. How do *I* know? Change the subject! Hold your ears! Run out of the room!

KATHRYN. (*Looks at him, absorbing this, for one beat; then surges for phone.*) I'm going to call a doctor—

JEREMY. I tell you, I'm all right—I never felt better—

KATHRYN. (*Okay, we'll play your game:*) Well, then, are you going in to the office, dear?

JEREMY. (*Caught:*) Oh. Oh, I—I guess so. Yes. I will. I suppose.

KATHRYN. (*With real concern.*) Jeremy, darling, *what* is making you so *nervous?* I've never in our whole life together seen you act this way.

JEREMY. You'd be nervous, too, if you had a dying man in your house— (*Remembers.*) and you have! So—please —don't mention the university to Charlie—

KATHRYN. All right, I promise.

JEREMY. Raise your right hand—

KATHRYN. (*Starts to do so, then yanks it down, pushed too far at this.*) Jeremy Troy, if you think—!

JEREMY. Okay, okay, I'm sorry. But remember, you

promised. (*Starts for front door.*) Is that cab still waiting?

KATHRYN. No, I let him go. I'll call you another one.

JEREMY. You don't have to do that—

KATHRYN. Yes I do. If you're going to be the nutsy husband, the least I can do is be the model wife.

JEREMY. (*Remembers.*) Model! Excuse me— (*Lurches across room toward kitchen doorway.*) but I have to use the car!

KATHRYN. What for?

JEREMY. To catch a bus! (*Exits into kitchen.*)

KATHRYN. (*Calls.*) But how am I going to do my shopping?

JEREMY. (*Off.*) We'll send out for pizza!

(*We hear back DOOR slam, on:*)

KATHRYN. Jeremy Troy—! (*Starts toward kitchen; stops as front door CHIMES sound; flings arms overhead in exasperation and starts for front door on:*) Now what? (*Exits through archway, opens door, steps back into view.*)

TINA. (*A trim little redhead, hair backswept into a bun, dark-rimmed glasses, carrying large purse, and bundled up in overcoat, enters.*) Is this the Jeremy Troy residence?

KATHRYN. Yes, it is . . .

TINA. (*Relieved, comes down into living room, undoing coat.*) I'm Tina Winslow, from the Left Bank.

KATHRYN. Oh? . . . Well—won't you come in? (*Belatedly shuts front door, comes down after* TINA, *during:*)

TINA. Thank you. My, what a pretty place! (*The coat comes off, revealing her in a bright yellow sleeveless dress, setting off a fantastic figure.*)

KATHRYN. Thank you very much— (*Repeating the name, as if to give it meaning for herself.*) Miss Winslow . . . ?

(*For the remainder of their scene, the effect is this:* TINA

is like a butterfly KATHRYN *can never quite pin
down, in her words and actions, babbling on in
friendly chattiness, moving here and there, undoing
her hair into a titian cascade, trying "poses" in the
light from the window, only really half-hearing*
KATHRYN *at all.*)

TINA. I'm so excited. This is my first real assignment.

KATHRYN. I don't understand. Is my husband *expecting* you?

TINA. Well, I hope so! He has to pay me for all the
time I'm here, whether he uses me or not.

KATHRYN. Could you—uh—make that just a little
clearer?

TINA. (*Starts unsnapping garters, rolling down and removing nylons.*) Well, you see, I get five dollars an hour.
That's not as much as the other girls get, but that's because I'm still an amateur. Do you have any idea how
long he wants me for?

KATHRYN. (*Too amazed at the nylon-doffing to react
with indignation.*) Young lady— Miss Winslow— Are
you sure you have the right house?

TINA. If this is five-thirty-one Pinecrest Drive. You
said it was the home of Jeremy Troy . . .

KATHRYN. And you say my husband sent for you?

TINA. (*Placing stockings neatly in bag, along with
shoes, and getting into fluffy slippers matching her dress.*)
Well, not me *personally*, if you know what I mean. He
just called and tried to get one of the regular girls, but
they were all out so he said he'd take anybody at all and
they decided I should have my first chance. I can really
use the experience. I'm so lucky he called just as I was
passing the switchboard—

KATHRYN. Switchboard?

TINA. Well, sure . . . What do you think we do, walk
the streets trying to get somebody interested? (*Laughs at
her little joke, as* KATHRYN *goggles.*)

KATHRYN. Are you telling me my husband uses your—
place of employment—on a regular basis—?!

TINA. I guess so, I mean, he called *us*, we didn't call *him*.

KATHRYN. There *must* be a mistake! *My* husband is a very successful lawyer in New York City—

TINA. What's that got to do with it? Every man should have a hobby. (*As* KATHRYN *reacts.*) Say—I wonder—could I trouble you for a cup of coffee? It's awfully cold outside, and I'm very susceptible—

KATHRYN. (*A haven of normalcy beckons amid all this madness.*) By all means. I could use a cup myself. (*Sits, pours two cupfuls as* TINA *sits beside her on sofa.* KATHRYN *takes fortifying sip, turns to get to the bottom of this thing.*) *Now*, Miss Winslow—

TINA. (*Has taken sip, too; reacts to strange flavor which* KATHRYN *is far too bemused to notice herself.*) Say—do you have any Coffeemate?

KATHRYN. (*Foiled in mid-purpose, echoes the word with resignation.*) Coffeemate. (*Gets up, starts doggedly toward kitchen.*)

TINA. (*Has taken second sip, found it not bad as she thought, gets up and follows* KATHRYN *as far as right archway, stands before fireplace, facing mostly Downstage, but speaking Off Right.*) You know, it's nice to meet a wife who's so broadminded.

KATHRYN. (*As she exits into kitchen.*) My dear Miss Winslow, if there is one thing I am *not*, it is broadminded. I am merely giving Jeremy the benefit of the doubt until I have heard *his* side of the story— (*Half a beat; then, despite herself, adds:*) and it had better be good!

TINA. Oh. Then you don't approve of his hobby?

KATHRYN. (*Off.*) If you care to put it mildly!

TINA. (*Prattling on, oblivious to the charged atmosphere.*) Some women would get terribly upset. Like my father, for example. He's very upset about my job, but— I'm over twenty-one and this is what I want to be, so he's given his grudging approval. I guess the main thing he objects to is when I take my clothes off. (*There is a CRASH of glass from the kitchen.*) Did you drop something? (*Ambles under archway;* CHARLIE *at that moment comes out of bathroom, crosses into guest room, shuts door; she hears door shut, comes out, peers up curiously as:*)

KATHRYN. (*Entering from kitchen with jagged jar-bottom.*) Yes-I-dropped-something! (*Hands it to her.*) Coffeemate! (*The pills are hitting her; she wobbles back to her seat on sofa.*)

TINA. Have I offended you somehow, Mrs. Troy?

KATHRYN. You have offended me, *and* how! The only reason you are not lying dead on the carpet is that I am saving myself for Jeremy!

TINA. Dead? But it's *only* five dollars . . . ?! (*Stares dismayed at broken jar, then sets it gingerly on mantel.*) This situation wasn't covered in my course of instruction . . . (*Yawns delicately.*) My, but it's *warm* in here! (*Blinks, sips coffee, wobbles down to sit beside* KATHRYN.)

KATHRYN. Not as warm as it's going to get when *Jeremy* comes home! No *wonder* he was jittery.

TINA. (*Almost weepily.*) I'm sorry you're so upset . . . Is it—is it the *money?*

KATHRYN. (*This aspect hadn't occurred to her, but it does now.*) Among other things—*yes!* (KATHRYN *turns to glare righteously at* TINA *after saying this line, when something unaccountable happens: a giggly laugh comes bubbling up, unbidden, and bursts tinkling from her lips; she blinks in surprise, but can't muster up anger; turning to cool decorum, instead, she is her most dignified as she continues:*) Would you like another coff of cuppee?

TINA. Yes, if you don't mind. I feel so terribly sleepy . . .

(*Watches, glassy-eyed, as* KATHRYN *fills her cup where it has been set down on the coffee table, then—without uptilting the spout—swings the pot the length of the table and refills her own cup, letting the interim-poured coffee lie in a spatter-line on the table.*)

KATHRYN. (*Sets down pot, solemnly feels flesh of* TINA'S *near upper arm.*) You know-- You *do* feel sleepy! (BOTH *nodding solemnly, they slowly burst into matched giggles, rock back limply toward opposite ends of sofa, subside, and:*) Well, if you get too tired, you can always sack out in our guest room.

TINA. (*Glasses a bit askew, removes them to peer myopically around, on:*) Where is it?

KATHRYN. (*Disdainfully.*) Don't play innocent with me— (*Beat; then, archly.*) I'll play by myself!

(BOTH *whoop giddily,* TINA *meanwhile rising with care and starting determinedly--but zigzaggedly—toward stairs.*)

TINA. (*Peers myopically.*) Which way are the stairs? I can't see a thing without my glasses.

KATHRYN. Then why don't— (*Yawns.*) —why don't you put them on?

TINA. All right. (*Yawns.*) Where are they?

KATHRYN. (*Squints.*) Try your left hand. (TINA *does, finds glasses, gets them on.*)

TINA. I feel so foolish. Can you imagine me going to bed on my first assignment?

KATHRYN. (*Watches her till she's up a few stairs; then:*) *I'll* say I can!

TINA. (*Half-flops over stair rail, sensing a possible slur:*) Would you mind explaining that remark?

KATHRYN. *Yes!*

(BOTH *laugh wildly,* TINA *continuing jauntily-if-wobbly upstairs,* KATHRYN *lolling back on sofa, studying coffee cup dangling by its handle from her thumb, as if utterly fascinated by this bauble.*)

TINA. (*Near bathroom door, leans limply over balcony rail for:*) Say . . . do you know if your husband plans to put me on a pedestal?

KATHRYN. (*With cheery resignation, and without look-*

ing upward, carols:) Well, if he *does*, you're one up on *me!*

(BOTH *laugh wildly; *TINA'S* laugh carries her hurtling into bathroom; door closes after her; *KATHRYN'S* laugh, as she breaks it again and again to catch her breath, slowly changes into heartbroken sobbing, and all at once she is wailing miserably as *CHARLIE—*in paint-daubed smock and matching pants—enters from guest room. He sees her as she sees him. She rises on:*)

CHARLIE. Kathryn—? (*Sensing something is amiss, hurries toward stairs, as:*)

KATHRYN. (*Reeling, starts a dead lunge toward foot of stairs.*) Charlie— Charlie Bickle from the university—am I ever glad to see *you!*

(CHARLIE *has broken speed records to do it, but he gets to foot of stairs, and her, just as she falls straight forward, and flops into his arms, so limp as to be apparently boneless.*)

CHARLIE. (*Staggering, half-dragging her toward sofa again.*) Kathryn! Kathryn, what's the matter?

KATHRYN. (*Perched briefly on sofa arm, flings up a hand to cry:*) Everything! (*Gesture carries her back supine on sofa for:*) Oh, Charlie! To think Jeremy could deceive me this way—a lie, a rotten lie, our whole life together!

CHARLIE. (*Glumly, thinking he understands.*) Oh. I see. Then he's told you.

KATHRYN. (*Struggles to perch upon sofa arm again.*) Ha! Fat chance of that! I had to find out for myself. 'Sfunny how a woman can live with a man—and think she knows him—and then— Wham!— (*Another extravagant gesture brings her to her feet in a limp pirouette which lets her fall backward, Left, into his arms.*) —the whole bottom drops out of everything!

CHARLIE. (*Stares at her dangling form in deep perplexity.*) Kathryn . . . aren't you taking this a little—*hard*? How much have you *had*, anyway?

KATHRYN. (*Raises back of hand up till it supports her chin.*) Right up to here!

CHARLIE. (*Gets her to her feet, so they face one another, she Left, he Right.*) I can believe it. But listen, this is no solution. Sure, Jeremy made a mistake. But he wouldn't have done it at all if he didn't love you so much—

KATHRYN. (*Fleetingly sobered.*) How's that again? (*Leans toward him to peer into his face, keeps leaning till he has to catch her again, on:*)

CHARLIE. It's true. He told me so himself. He did the whole thing for love of you. It's been a long and terrible struggle for him.

KATHRYN. Now, just a minute— Do you mean to say you don't think this is the worst thing that could happen in a marriage?

(*Has chest-thumped him backward for emphasis, and he suddenly sprawls backward over sofa-arm, on:*)

CHARLIE. Of course not! (*Sees KATHRYN is still toppling his way; rolls to safety on:*) I mean, all he did was practice a little deception—

(*On hands and knees behind coffee table as she flops face down onto sofa, starts getting to his feet during:*)

KATHRYN. (*A mumble lost in the cushions:*) You call it *little?* (*CHARLIE stares, grunts curiously, lifts her face so he can hear:*) You call it *little!* I was never so shocked in my life!

CHARLIE. But don't you see? He wanted to make an impression on you—

KATHRYN. (*More a shudder than a laugh:*) Oh-ho-ho, he did—he made an impression, all right! (*Now up on hands and knees on sofa, lurches toward coffee pot.*) I need more coffee.

CHARLIE. (*Catches her, gets her seated on sofa.*) *I'll* get it! I'll get it. (*As he pours cup of coffee,* KATHRYN *tries to get off sofa, Left, ends up seated on arm again, feet dangling above floor, head almost resting on knees;* CHARLIE *turns with coffee, rushes around her, drops on Downstage knee to face her, and starts to gently feed her sip after sip of coffee, during:*) Try to see Jeremy's point of view in this thing. Here he is, a man with a dull, uninteresting job. Then he meets a girl, a sweet, young, loving girl. He falls for her, hard. He wants her. He has to have her, no matter what, even if it means practicing a life of deception. Because, she's something special!

KATHRYN. (*Now very bewildered.*) But I understood— I mean—this isn't the same sweet innocent girl he *started* with—?

CHARLIE. (*Gently, fondly.*) Oh, yes. Yes it is. No matter what changes the years may have wrought, this is still the same girl he's always loved. And I can honestly say I approve.

KATHRYN. (*An arctic chill even amid the fuzziness:*) Oh, you *approve*, do you—?

CHARLIE. Take the word of an artist, Kathryn. I have an eye for lovely things. I think that Jeremy's a very lucky man—

(*And* KATHRYN'S *Downstage arm suddenly comes up with a fist on the end of it, in a roundhouse uppercut that sends* CHARLIE *sprawling onto his back before the fireplace, out cold; the follow-through of the blow brings her to her feet and headed toward the stairs, and she scrambles up them monkey-like on hands and feet, growling like a wild woman, pausing at the top of the flight to shout down at him:*)

KATHRYN. You damn four-letter men are all alike! (*Lurches into bedroom, slams door.*)

JEREMY. (*Off, Left:*) Coffee! *Coffee!* (*Bursts into house through front door, down into living room, on:*) Kathryn, don't drink the— (*Sees* CHARLIE; *stops; then stoops, lifts wrist and notes cup still dangling from his limp fingers.*) Aha! It worked!

(*Drops arm to floor, rushes to coffee pot, lifts lid, reacts to lack of contents with horror, slams lid on, rushes back to* CHARLIE, *takes his pulse, sighs with relief; then hefts him under arms, starts to drag him backward toward archway.*)

CHARLIE. (*Blearily.*) Um. Huh. Hey— What the hell d'ya think y're doin'?

JEREMY. (*Shocked, lets go, rushes back for second look into pot.*) Charlie, you're not out!

CHARLIE. (*Mumbling dazedly, massaging jaw.*) Out? Out cold! She knocked me cold—

JEREMY. (*Not even hearing.*) But the whole *pot's* gone! How can you be awake?

CHARLIE. (*Swaying like a sailor on a tossing deck, holding jaw, comes down.*) Jeremy— I got three things to tell you about your wife: *One,* she's got a hell of a right cross, *two,* she knows, *three,* everything!

JEREMY. (*Still on his own tack.*) Charlie, I don't get it: I put almost a full bottle of tranquillizers in this coffee and you're not out—

CHARLIE. (*Blinking to awareness.*) In—*that* pot, Jeremy—?

JEREMY. (*Short, sheepish laugh:*) Yeah. I was going to stash you in the cellar till after dinner—

CHARLIE. (*A laugh of self-reproof.*) And *I* thought she'd been hitting the *bottle*— (*Laugh freezes on face, then panic takes its place.*) Jeremy— *Kathryn's* been drinking that coffee!

JEREMY. Omigosh! Where *is* she?

CHARLIE. (*Aghast to realize.*) I don't *know!*

(*There is instant pandemonium: With* CHARLIE *shouting "Kathryn!" and* JEREMY *shouting "Kathy!," in ad-lib repetition, the* MEN *run all over the place, looking out on the front porch, in the windowseat, up the chimney, in a desk-drawer, etc., till finally they*

*rush behind the fireplace from opposite sides, cry out
in twin grunts of pain, and stagger back into view,
clutching foreheads.)*

JEREMY. Upstairs!
CHARLIE. (*Moving ahead of him.*) Quick! (*Gallops upstairs.*)
JEREMY. (*Following him.*) I'll never forgive myself
if— Kathy!

(*They dash into the two bedrooms, CHARLIE choosing
correctly.*)

CHARLIE. (*Off.*) I've got her! (*Enters balcony, carrying a rag-limp KATHRYN in his arms.*)
JEREMY. (*Rushes to him, and they rotate around her
in a circle, holding her.*) Listen, *I* can manage her. You
run downstairs and makes a fresh pot of coffee—I'll bring
her down.
CHARLIE. (*Tries to descend, can't.*) Gimme my *arm*
back. (*Tugs arm from under her, dashes downstairs.*)
JEREMY. (*Descending clumsily, KATHRYN sagging
lower and lower in his arms:*) Kathryn! Kathy, darling,
wake up! Please wake up! Ice cubes! Charlie, bring me
ice cubes! We'll put them down her back—
CHARLIE. (*By now off in kitchen, pops back in for:*)
You ought to call your doctor—
JEREMY. (*At foot of stairs, crossing toward center.*)
We don't have a regular doctor—we've always been so
damned healthy!

(*Sits her on floor, hefts her to her feet, as CHARLIE pops
back into kitchen, returning seconds later with tray
of ice cubes.*)

CHARLIE Here they are—how many do you want?
JEREMY. All of them! Here, I'll hold her . . . (*He is
facing Upstage, now, at Center, KATHRYN's sweetly slumbering face visible over his shoulder, on which her chin
rests.*) you put them down her back—
CHARLIE. Here goes. Boy, are they *cold!* (*Gingerly
drops a few down neck of her dress.*)

KATHRYN. (*Instantly awake, popeyed and shrieking, leaping straight up.*) Stop! Stop it! What are you doing? Let me go! (*The shrieks become hilarious giggles.*)

JEREMY. It's for your own good, darling. More, Charlie, more! (CHARLIE *unzips back of dress at neck, dumps rest of tray inside.*)

KATHRYN. Have you two gone crazy? Stop it—what's the matter with you?

CHARLIE. That's all of them—shall I make some more?

JEREMY. No! Coffee—as strong as possible!

KATHRYN. (*As* CHARLIE *dashes into kitchen again.*) Jeremy! Let me go! Jeremeeeee—! (*Wrenches free, wriggling madly, laughing wildly.*)

JEREMY. That's it, darling: Don't stand still—keep moving!

(*Amid flying ice cubes,* KATHRYN *is doing just that, like a go-go girl gone berserk; then, in mid-paroxysm, sights on* JEREMY, *and launches a wide-swinging punch at his head; he ducks, the spin twirls her about, and she falls back into his arms just as* CHARLIE *rushes from kitchen with a full coffee cup in his two hands.*)

CHARLIE. I found a jar of instant—

JEREMY. (*Struggling to hold a writhing wife.*) Quick, give it to her! (CHARLIE *force-feeds* KATHRYN; *she swallows, then stiffens like a ramrod canted against* JEREMY, *who rocks her to a vertical stance; when she just stands there, mouth guppying and eyes popping:*) How much instant did you *put* in that, anyhow?

CHARLIE. Half a cup of powder to half a cup of water. I thought it'd speed things up.

JEREMY. (*As* KATHRYN, *still gasping, gropes her way to sofa, follows with:*) Feeling better, darling?

KATHRYN. (*Sitting, slowly coming out of shock, more heartbroken than angry.*) Better? I wasn't feeling bad at *all* till you two *maniacs* started in on me. At least—not physically . . . (*Tries to smooth dress as* CHARLIE *scurries about collecting fallen ice cubes and replacing them in tray.*) Oh, Jeremy—! What hurts me the worst of all is the deception. All these years—living with a stranger—and I didn't know it!

JEREMY. I'm sorry, darling. I—I was *afraid* to tell you the truth—

CHARLIE. (*Prodding tender jaw.*) You had good reason to be— (*Exits to kitchen with tray and ice cubes.*)

JEREMY. Well . . . Where do we go from here, Kathy?

KATHRYN. I wish I knew. If—maybe if you had told me —had only told me when it first happened—we could have— I mean—*one* mistake is bad enough, but if you had been really sorry for it—but—to keep it *up*, year after year after *year*—

JEREMY. (*Has been hovering solicitously; now turns away dejectedly.*) What can I say? I did it. There's no changing that fact. (CHARLIE *re-enters from kitchen in time to hear:*) I guess it's all too far gone for apologies—

CHARLIE. No, don't say that! No matter what a man has done, if his wife cares for him at all, she offers her help, not her scorn. Don't make a hasty decision, please. There's no problem too tough for two intelligent people in open, honest discussion.

KATHRYN. (*Confused, covers face, shakes head, rises.*) Before we do *anything*, I'm going to dry my neck! (*Lost and bewildered, exits into kitchen.*)

CHARLIE. (*Admiringly.*) Jeremy-boy, you've got yourself a real woman there! Now all you have to do is sell her on the idea of your going to night school, and your troubles are over.

JEREMY. It's too late. It's all over. You saw her face. Nothing I promise is going to change that.

CHARLIE. Don't worry, old buddy. Charlie is here. I'll sell her on the night school idea, you just watch—

JEREMY. Charlie, I can't believe you don't have some kind of an angle.

CHARLIE. Of *course* I've got an angle— (*Grips* JEREMY'S *shoulder with one hand, points dramatically toward kitchen with the other.*) I'm not going to let that woman break up our home! (KATHRYN *appears in kitchen doorway.*) Ssh, here she comes. Leave everything to me.

(*Turns toward the entering* KATHRYN, *opens mouth to speak, but she walks right by him to her coat and purse on desk chair.*)

JEREMY. Kathy . . . where are you going?

KATHRYN. Anywhere!

JEREMY. Darling, don't go. I'll change my ways. I'm sorry I got you so upset. I apologize!

KATHRYN. Ha! (*Tries to get to front door, but he blocks her path.*) Get out of my way, or I won't be responsible for my actions!

CHARLIE. Kathryn, be reasonable—

KATHRYN. *Reasonable?*

CHARLIE. You said what hurt the most was the deception, right? So—now that you know the truth, your basic objection is all taken care of, huh?

JEREMY. Yes! That's right! And, so long as I tell you the truth from now on, everything's fine, hmm?

KATHRYN. You're crazy—both of you are stark, staring crazy. Any forgiving of Jeremy would be conditional to his not going *on* with this thing any more—I hope *that's* not too difficult for you to grasp!

JEREMY. Well, naturally! And I promise you, darling, that I will rectify the situation just as soon as possible.

(CHARLIE *nods his support of the plan vigorously.*)

KATHRYN. Hold on— What do you mean, as soon as possible?

CHARLIE. Well, it's not the sort of thing that can be rectified overnight.

KATHRYN. Oh? And why not, may I ask?

CHARLIE. Well—I—um— It's a complicated affair, Kathryn—

JEREMY. Yes, darling. It may take me *years* to get out of it—

KATHRYN. *Years?*

CHARLIE. Certainly. Night after night—

JEREMY. —out to all hours—
CHARLIE. —staggering home red-eyed and weary—
KATHRYN. I never *heard* such an outrageous suggestion!
(*Backs away from them, toward now-clear Left archway.*)
JEREMY. But darling, I was counting on your help—
KATHRYN. (*Stops in archway, thunderstruck.*) *Help?*
JEREMY. Certainly! If you don't get a part-time job,
how can I *afford* it?

(KATHRYN *gives an incoherent scream, lurches from sight,
and we hear the slam of the front DOOR; the two*
MEN *just stand, numb.*)

CHARLIE. Well . . . what can I say?
JEREMY. Damned if I know. I never, in all my wildest
nightmares of discovery, thought she'd take it *this* hard.
CHARLIE. Yeah. I never saw anyone get *so* angry so
fast.

(*Each lost in his own thoughts, they are coming down to
sofa and sitting, puzzled and bemused by the unexpected hurricane.*)

JEREMY. You know what baffles me more than anything? *How* she found out! It's downright supernatural.

(*Unnoticed by either,* TINA *enters from bathroom, somewhat recovered; she sees the two* MEN, *adjusts her
glasses and pats her hair, then descends slowly to
living room, during:*)

CHARLIE. Let's think it through, logically.
JEREMY. Okay. Now, fact number one: Kathryn knows.
CHARLIE. Right!
JEREMY. So, if she knows, someone told her.
CHARLIE. Exactly!
JEREMY. Now, *I* certainly didn't tell her . . . and the
only *other* person who knew *is*—
CHARLIE. (*Sees where logic is heading; groans.*) Aw,
c'mon, Jer! *I* didn't tell her—why *would* I?

JEREMY. (*Realizes truth of this, ponders a second; then:*) Maybe you told her inadvertently . . . maybe you let something slip—some phrase that gave her a clue—

CHARLIE. What clue? Let's be logical. She wasn't mad when she left with your brief—

JEREMY. That's true . . . and she wasn't mad when she got back, or even later, when I left the house—

CHARLIE. Yet by the time I'd finished my shower she knew everything—

JEREMY. Okay! Now—what happened between the time I went out and you got your clothes back on?

TINA. (*Now at foot of stairs.*) Hi, there! (*Her face, figure, and inappropriate good cheer are dazzling; both* MEN *look at her, at one another, then—slightly shocked —straight out front, rising slowly to their feet, then back at her.*) I'm Tina Winslow . . . (*Both* MEN *remain mute, but move toward her;* CHARLIE *brings the hassock Downstage Center, gestures for her to approach it; she does.*) What's the matter? (*She sits, looking up at these two hovering vultures.*) Why are you looking at me like that? (*The silence is ominous; panic sets in, and she rises uneasily on:*) Who are you two, anyway—?

(*Each* MAN *drops a hand firmly on each of her shoulders before her rise is complete, and they press her gently back upon her perch.*)

CHARLIE. I'm Charlie Bickle, and this is Jeremy Troy.

TINA. (*Relieved, turns to* JEREMY.) Oh, you're the one who hired me to pose.

JEREMY. I never. Charlie's the Rembrandt. He's just staying with us temporarily.

TINA. (*Laughs with amused chagrin.*) Oh, well, no *wonder* your wife was upset! (*Both* MEN *react, lean closer.*) I told her *you* were the one, and she seemed quite put out about it. Mostly I guess it was the money. Is she on a tight budget or something?

JEREMY. (*Jumps in quickly as she stops for breath.*) Listen—think back, Miss Winslow . . . When did my wife start to get upset?

CHARLIE. What did you say to her?

TINA. (*Thinks deeply, realizes she must re-enact to remember, gets up and hurries Upstage to Left archway, the two* MEN *trailing her—now and throughout her narrative —like loping bloodhounds, eager to keep on the scent of their quarry.*) I came in . . . I told her my name, and that I was from the Left Bank . . . gave her my coat . . . she hung it up . . . (*Shakes head in frowning concentration.*) She certainly wasn't mad *then*—

CHARLIE. So far so good!

JEREMY. Then what happened?

TINA. (*Hurries to sofa, on:*) She offered me a cup of coffee, and then— (*Stops, elated.*) *Now* I remember! (*Rushes Upstage Right, whirls in archway to face them, points finger out into kitchen accusingly.*) All at once—as we were talking—*she* dropped the Coffeemate! (*Folds arms in triumph, nods once, firmly.*)

(*Both* MEN *turn Downstage, hands clasped behind backs, slightly slouching as they walk ruminatively Downstage, on:*)

JEREMY *and* CHARLIE. (*Ad-lib echoing word, as though it's a meaningful clue.*) Coffeemate . . . Coffeemate . . . !

(JEREMY *stops below desk, and* CHARLIE *below sofa, as:*)

TINA. (*Rushing eagerly down to confront* CHARLIE, *her back to* JEREMY.) Say, you know, this is exciting? (*He comes out of his reverie to look at her, and for the first time realizes that this is a lovely girl, indeed, before him; the* TWOSOME *are aware only of one another till* JEREMY'S *cry.*) It's just like one of those plays on TV about a murder—

JEREMY. Excuse me—

TINA. That's my ambition, some day!

CHARLIE. Murder?

TINA. No, silly! TV!

JEREMY. Young lady—

TINA. I want to be an actress. A lot of very famous actresses started as models.

JEREMY. Miss Winslow—

TINA. (*As she and* CHARLIE *sink onto sofa, leaning their sides against the back to better face one another, all settled down snug and cozy for a cheerful chat:*) Maybe if I'm lucky I'll even wind up in the movies—

JEREMY. (*Brings them both back guiltily on their feet facing him, with cry:*) Please! (*As terrified* TINA *cowers against* CHARLIE, *both facing* JEREMY.) Let's—get back to my wife, okay? What did you say to her that might make her drop the Coffeemate?

TINA. (*Guided by* CHARLIE, *comes thoughtfully back to perch on hassock, seated between the two hovering* MEN *as before; then, brightly:*) I *remember!* I was just telling her about my father and how he objects to my taking my clothes off.

JEREMY. But—then you must have already told her you were an artist's model. I thought, maybe . . .

CHARLIE. Thought what, Jeremy?

JEREMY. Well, Kathryn was a bit peeved about your staying with us, and I thought finding out you'd hired a model was the last straw.

TINA. But I didn't *know* I was here for *him.* I said it was *you.*

JEREMY. Even so, if Kathryn knew what Miss Winslow was—

CHARLIE. (*The dawn of horror:*) Jeremy— *Did* Kathryn know what Miss Winslow was?

TINA. Of course she did. Why, even before I took off my stockings I said I was from the Left Bank—

JEREMY. (*Beginning to get the picture, takes a slow step backward, on:*) And—you said *I* sent for you—

CHARLIE. (*A backward step of his own.*) And you told her you charged five dollars an hour—

TINA. (*Brightly.*) And I said every man should have a hobby.

(*Both* MEN *recoil violently, turning away and covering faces;* CHARLIE *recovers first, looks ruefully at* JEREMY, *on:*)

CHARLIE. And *you* said, "I apologize!"

JEREMY. (*Glassy-eyed with the truth.*) I'm lucky I didn't say, "Boys will be boys!"

CHARLIE. (*Snaps fingers, then crosses to* JEREMY, *on:*) Jeremy! Hold on! Don't you realize what this means? My friend, you are a very fortunate young man—

JEREMY. You mean because Kathryn left here without killing me?

CHARLIE. No! Don't you see—Kathryn was hovering on the brink of forgiving you about Miss Winslow. If she could even *consider* forgiving a thing like that, she'll never bat an eye when you tell her about your *law degree.*

TINA. (*Still perched demurely on hassock.*) Oh, but she *knows* about *that*—

JEREMY and CHARLIE. (*Whirl, lunge toward her on:*) She *does?*

TINA. Well, sure! She *told* me you were a *lawyer.*

JEREMY. (*Gets back on track again with an effort.*) Charlie, you're right! All I have to do is find Kathryn, tell her the truth, and everything's rosy again. My little home—my little wife—my little partnership— (*Gasps.*) Ivorsen! He's due at seven—can we *find* Kathryn by then?

CHARLIE. (*With no optimism at all.*) Well, I suppose you could start phoning hotels—?

JEREMY. (*False start toward phone; stops in despair.*) We'd *never* be able to check them all out in time—

CHARLIE. Then what're you going to do?

JEREMY. (*Pacing, distraught.*) I don't know—I honestly

don't know. (*A cry to heaven.*) Just one lousy little perfect evening—that's all I ask of my destiny! But—*how?* How can I *possibly—?*

(*His eye falls on* TINA; *he stares at her, shrewdly; then he smiles; nervously,* TINA *smiles back;* CHARLIE, *who started to sit on sofa during* JEREMY'S *woeful diatribe, rises apprehensively.*)

CHARLIE. Jeremy . . . What are you thinking—?
TINA. Mr. Troy— You look so—so strange. . . .
JEREMY. (*Advancing slowly on her.*) Listen— You say you want to be an actress? (*She nods, her frozen smile growing uneasy.*) How would you like to play the part of my wife?

(CHARLIE *groans, covers eyes, sinks with a thud onto sofa.*)

TINA. (*Humoring a maniac, keeps smiling, facing him, as her feet sidle slowly around hassock to the side farthest from his looming form.*) I don't think so. Really. I don't think so. (*Now rises and follows her feet away from him across the room.*) Can I go home now?
JEREMY. (*Lopes lightning-fast to block her path.*) Just for a few hours this evening! All you'd have to do is fix a meal, serve it, and be charming.

(CHARLIE, *face still hidden, shudders and groans hopelessly.*)

TINA. (*Looking from huddled* CHARLIE *to hovering* JEREMY.) N-no, I don't want to get mixed up in any funny business—
JEREMY. Not even for—*ten* dollars an hour?
TINA. (*Completes half a headshake, then widens eyes, very tempted.*) Does—does that include the time it'll take to cook?

JEREMY. (*Sees his advantage and presses it, moving toward her.*) It includes every moment from the time you arrived here today un'il Mister Ivorsen goes home tonight —with a hundred-dollar guaranteed *minimum*—

(TINA *squeals in delight, and starts pat-a-caking her hands;* CHARLIE *cannot stand any more; he surges wildly to his feet.*)

CHARLIE. Don't do it, girl. If you have any brains at all, run for your life, right now.

(TINA *reacts, startled back to her senses;* JEREMY *descends to* CHARLIE, *pleadingly but determinedly.*)

JEREMY. Charlie, have a heart! What's one tiny little lie?

(TINA, *during their exchange, nervously gets coat, bag, etc., and starts tiptoeing toward front door.*)

CHARLIE. Think of all the trouble your *last* one caused you. Besides, Ivorsen knows what Kathryn looks like—
JEREMY. No, they've never met—
CHARLIE. Kathryn took Ivorsen that brief—
JEREMY. She sent it with a cab driver. Stop fighting, Charlie!
CHARLIE. But think—even if you *do* get through tonight, Ivorsen is *bound* to run into Kathryn *some* day—
JEREMY. Yeah, but once I'm a full partner, what can he *do* me? (*Chortles in triumph, whirls, sees departing* TINA.) *Hey!*
TINA. (*Trapped, whirls, blurts inanely:*) Goodbye, you two! It was real nice meeting you. Both. (*Starts through Left archway.*)
JEREMY. (*One step after her.*) But what about your movie career?
TINA. (*Draws herself up icily, in archway, holds for:*)

This kind of experience I don't need. (*Whirls, exits through front door, leaving it open.*)

JEREMY. (*Rushes into archway, remains in view there as he shouts:*) Too bad, Miss Winslow! This is the first time I ever heard of an aspiring actress turning down a chance to audition for a real Hollywood talent scout. (*Comes Downstage to* CHARLIE, *chuckling insidiously.*) I give her exactly twenty seconds!

CHARLIE. Jeremy, you said just *one* more lie. Besides, nobody in their right *mind* believes in talent scouts, these days—

JEREMY. She hasn't *got* a mind!

CHARLIE. But where the hell are you going to *get* the talent scout—? (*Sees the gleam in* JEREMY's *eye, realizes, recoils.*) *Oh, noooooo!*

JEREMY. (*Very lawyer-like, drives each point home like a hammer-blow:*) Why not? Look at it this way, Charlie: Why am I going to be in big trouble tonight when Ivorsen arrives?

CHARLIE. Because Kathryn's not here---

JEREMY. And why isn't she here?

CHARLIE. Because of Miss Winslow—

JEREMY. And *who* sent for *Miss Winslow—?*

(*As* CHARLIE *gapes, speechless,* TINA *dashes into house, agog.*)

TINA. A real Hollywood talent scout, Mister Troy—? *Who?*

CHARLIE. (*Beat; then succumbs glumly to an inevitable fate, sighing:*) Don't just stand there, baby; lemme see your legs!

(JEREMY *beams triumphantly, and* CHARLIE *sags, as* TINA *does so, and:*)

THE CURTAIN FALLS

ACT TWO

The Troy home, about 7 o'clock that evening. The paint-
ing over the mantel is still Charlie's creation, but
now flanked by the graduation photo and the di-
ploma, in matching frames. The drapes are drawn
across the window, Right. JEREMY, *in a brown tweed*
suit, is on the phone at the desk, a phone book, with
the yellow pages open, before him. During his open-
ing speech, CHARLIE *will enter, resplendent in a*
tuxedo, trot down the stairs, and start out toward the
kitchen.

JEREMY. Yes, Mrs. Kathryn Troy, T-r-o-y . . . She
would have registered sometime today . . . Oh . . .
You're sure? . . . All right. Thanks, anyways. (*Hangs up,*
slams phone book shut in disgust, then sees CHARLIE.)
Charlie, this dinner isn't formal.

CHARLIE. (*Without breaking stride.*) It is, now!

JEREMY. (*Rises, realizing:*) Hey, that's my tux. What
are you doing in my tux?

CHARLIE. (*Stops, turns.*) Your other stuff didn't fit me.
(*Lifts trouser-legs to expose white anklets.*) I couldn't
find any black socks, though. (*The PHONE rings.*) Telephone, Jeremy.

JEREMY. Now, listen here, Charlie— (*PHONE rings*
again.)

CHARLIE. *Tel*-e-phone!

JEREMY. It's Kathryn! (*Turns, grabs up phone:*)
Hello, darling? . . . Oh . . . Yes, just a minute . . .
(*Calls.*) Tina! Telephone!

TINA. (*Bustles in from kitchen, removing apron, in*
gorgeous dress.) Who is it?

JEREMY. (*With resignation.*) Your *father* again!

48

TINA. Oh, gee, I'm sorry. (*Takes phone from him, sighs into it:*) Hi, Pop! . . . No, everything's fine, just fine! . . . Well of *course* I've got my clothes on!

(JEREMY *has been crossing toward* CHARLIE, *who is peeking out between the drapes at the night, but both* MEN *react to her line and turn to look at her; she shrugs at them, helplessly.*)

JEREMY. (*Turns back to face* CHARLIE.) Listen, *something* of mine must fit you besides that tux!

CHARLIE. Well, there's always your bathing suit . . . How informal *is* this dinner?

TINA. (*Recaptures their attention with:*) Honestly, Pop, he doesn't want a model, he needs a wife— (*Suddenly sniffs air.*) Hey, I've got to go, now. 'Bye! (*Hangs up, turns to two* MEN, *announces:*) I think the lettuce is burning! (*Exits swiftly into kitchen.*)

JEREMY. (*As it sinks in.*) The *lettuce* is burning . . . ?

CHARLIE. (*With insouciant aplomb.*) That's what happens if you don't keep stirring it—

(CHARLIE *turns, and as he exits to kitchen, door CHIMES sound;* JEREMY, *galvanized, rushes toward front door.*)

JEREMY. Coming, sir! Coming!

(*Admits* IVORSEN, *a big beefy middle-aged man in expensive coat and hat;* IVORSEN *comes down into living room, doffs coat on:*)

IVORSEN. Evening, Jeremy! Boy, did you ever see such a rotten day? (*Stands revealed in tuxedo fully as resplendent as* CHARLIE'S.)

JEREMY. (*Reacts to it, on:*) Never! . . . Here, let me take your things, sir. (*While he hangs them up, and* IVORSEN *idly scans painting.*) I'm sorry your wife couldn't be with you tonight, sir.

IVORSEN. Audrey? Ha! She doesn't remember the *color* of snow any more. My wife won't leave Miami from Hallowe'en till May Day! She won't rest till they make her an honorary palm tree!

(*Chuckles;* JEREMY *realizes it's a joke, chuckles too, then:*)

JEREMY. Did you have any trouble finding the house, sir?

IVORSEN. Nope. Just brushed aside the snowdrifts, and there it was! (*Laughs again;* JEREMY *follows suit; then:*) But where is the little woman? I've been looking forward to meeting her.

JEREMY. Oh, she's right in the middle of dinner, sir.

IVORSEN. (*Laying the joke in with a heavy hand.*) Then—I hope she's wearing a wash-and-wear dress!

(*Same laugh business; then* JEREMY, *eager to escape the barrage of laughter-imperatives, starts for kitchen.*)

JEREMY. I'll just tell her you're here . . . Oh, Kathryn! Kathryn, darling! (*Almost collides with* CHARLIE, *who enters from kitchen bearing two drinks on a tray.*)

CHARLIE. Kathryn's still busy.

JEREMY. Oh, sir, this is—

CHARLIE. I'm Charles Bickle. I heard your hearty laughter, and I said to Mrs. Troy, "Now, there's a man who'd like to be sipping a dry martini!"

IVORSEN. Now that's what I call insight! (*As* JEREMY *gives up and exits to kitchen:*) Friend of the family?

CHARLIE. So far.

(BOTH MEN *sip drinks;* CHARLIE *stops after first sip, then goggles as he watches* IVORSEN *drain entire drink, and replace it with finality on the tray* CHARLIE *still holds.*)

IVORSEN. Mm, that hit the spot.

CHARLIE. (*Staring at size of emptied glass.*) Practically demolished it!

IVORSEN. (*Turns to him, then sees* JEREMY *entering with martini of his own.*) Oh, here you are again, Jeremy! How's our dinner doing?

JEREMY. As well as can be expected.

(TINA *enters from kitchen, arms outflung, trips gaily down to right of sofa, the better to face the trio, and strikes a very overdone pose of welcome: And for the rest of the play, all her lines* [*when she is "being Kathryn"*] *are spoken in the drawl of an amateur-theatrical southern belle; butter wouldn't melt on her cornpone.*)

TINA. Why, Mis-ter Ivorsen! So *you* are Jeremy's employer? Well, this is indeed an honor, sir.

(*As* CHARLIE *and* JEREMY *stare, horrified by their too-late realization of how* TINA *thinks one impresses a talent scout,* IVORSEN *gallantly r ses to take* TINA's *out-stretched hand; and as soon as he does, she curtsies, brings the back of his hand to her lips, and kisses it with a resounding smack;* IVORSEN *reacts, stares in bewilderment at the two* MEN.)

JEREMY. She—she's very class-conscious, sir!

IVORSEN. (*Accepting this, turns back to* TINA.) My dear, such a charming old-world drawl . . . where are you from?

TINA. Toronto.

(JEREMY, *simultaneously with* CHARLIE.)

JEREMY. Toronto, Ala-   CHARLIE. Toronto, Mis-
bama!   sissippi!

(*They look at one another, switch:*)

JEREMY. Toronto, Mississippi!   CHARLIE. Toronto, Alabama!

(A last look, and last switch:)

JEREMY. Toronto, Alabama!   CHARLIE. Toronto, Mississippi!

TINA. (*Eager to help:*) We lived in a trailer—

IVORSEN. Oh. I see—

CHARLIE. You *do?*

JEREMY. (*To* TINA, *desperately:*) I'm starved!

TINA. Well, little old dinner will be ready in just two shakes of a possum's tail!

(Trilling a coy laugh, she exits to kitchen; before IVORSEN *turns back to them,* CHARLIE *and* JEREMY *drain their drinks.)*

IVORSEN. Why, Jeremy! She's charming, utterly charming—a wife like that is worth her weight in gold—

CHARLIE. (*Looks automatically at wrist watch.*) Darn near!

JEREMY. Charlie, would you go out and give Kathryn a— (*Stops short of "—good swift kick!," controls himself for:*) a *hand* with things? See how the hors d'oeuvres are coming.

IVORSEN. Don't forget— One if by land, two if by sea! (*Roars at own joke;* CHARLIE *forces matching laugh, gives* JEREMY *an eloquent look of pain, exits with three empty glasses and tray.*) Say, I *like* that friend of yours. . . . Don't *you* own a dress suit?

JEREMY. Nobody told me dinner was formal. Besides, I lent mine to an artist friend, and he hasn't returned it yet.

IVORSEN. People in the arts simply cannot be trusted. By the way, what does *Charlie* do for a living?

JEREMY. (*Opens mouth, realizes "painter" and "talent scout" are now hazards.*) He—uh—um—

IVORSEN. Well?

JEREMY. (*Fishing for a safe vocation.*) What would *you* have become if you hadn't gone into *law?*

IVORSEN. A Presbyterian.

JEREMY. I mean, what line of *work,* sir?

IVORSEN. You don't mean to tell me that he's . . . an orthodontist?

JEREMY. Yes! That's what he is—

IVORSEN. How splendid! There's nothing I admire more than men of science who still retain a sense of beauty.

JEREMY. (*As* CHARLIE *enters from kitchen with plate of hors d'oeuvres.*) Oh, that's Charlie, all right: He lives for loveliness!

IVORSEN. (*As* CHARLIE *offers plate, and he and* JEREMY *help themselves.*) Say, Charlie, Jeremy was just telling me what you do for a living. You know, I admire your work tremendously. (CHARLIE *looks toward painting, smiles back at* IVORSEN, *pleased.*) I wonder if you'd be interested in working on *me,* some time?

CHARLIE. Well— Are you sure you can sit *still* long enough?

IVORSEN. Shouldn't be too difficult if you just fitted me with a *brace!* I've always wanted a dazzling smile.

CHARLIE. Well, if you've got the patience, I've got the white paint.

(IVORSEN *and a hapless* JEREMY *roar with laughter, as* CHARLIE *stares.*)

IVORSEN. Oh, that's good, very good! . . . But, seriously—*you're* the one with the patients! (*Same business.*) Don't you get it, Doc?

CHARLIE. (*With confused glance at* JEREMY *for help.*) I'm still working on the white paint—

IVORSEN. (*Roars again;* JEREMY *joins him;* CHARLIE *echoes them, uncertainly.*) Say, Jeremy—I'd like to wash up before dinner . . . ?

JEREMY. Oh, certainly, sir. Straight up the stairs, end of the balcony.

IVORSEN. (*Starts up, pauses halfway up flight.*) Never had to wash up so bad in all my life! (*Roars; they echo him, obediently, as he crosses to bathroom; then:*) Charlie— While I'm gone—don't try to *pull any fast ones!* (*Pantomimes tooth-pull on this, exits laughing into bathroom.*)

CHARLIE. (*Laughs till door shuts; then, quite seriously, to* JEREMY:) Does that bathroom door lock from the *outside?*

JEREMY. Oh, he's not so bad once you get to know him, Charlie, believe me—

CHARLIE. Believe *you?* For all *I* know, that's not even Mister *Ivorsen!*

JEREMY. Oh, sure it is. He's just a little mixed up because I told him you were an orthodontist.

(*On their next lines,* TINA *enters from kitchen, wheeling a table set for four, takes it to Downstage Left.*)

CHARLIE. What the hell did you tell him *that* for?

JEREMY. I had to: You're wearing my dress suit!

TINA. (*Flings arms wide in dramatic proclamation.*) Little old dinner is *served!* (*Accent goes normal, on:*) Hey, where'd he go?

JEREMY. Tina, for pete's sake, don't drop out of character like that—

TINA. Oh, then you *like* my accent!

JEREMY. No, but it's too late to change it, now—

CHARLIE. Tina, why are you *doing* the deep south dialect, anyhow?

TINA. The only other dialect I know is Spanish. (*To* JEREMY.) *Your* wife's not Spanish.

CHARLIE. She's got you there.

JEREMY. My stomach's sick!

TINA. (*Almost as if preceding line with "If you think it's sick,* now.") *Wait'll* you see what's for *dinner!*

CHARLIE. You'd better hurry. Ivorsen'll be down any minute. (*As* TINA *exits hurriedly to kitchen, remarks to* JEREMY:) Unless you're chickening out?

JEREMY. Of course not! We'll fill him full of food and liquor and send him chuckling off into the night, and then we can all sit back and relax.

CHARLIE. That's the insidious thing about your schemes, Jeremy—they all sound so plausible until they're tried.

JEREMY. But what can possibly go wrong?

(With a whiz of wind and snow and a door-slam, KATH-RYN appears in Left archway.)

CHARLIE. I rest my case! *(Exits almost at a gallop to the safety of the kitchen.)*

JEREMY. *(Flings arms wide, rushes toward her, on:)* Kathryn, darling, you've come *back* to me— *(Completes motion by flinging arms wider, half-crouching, as he stops before her, and screams piteously:)* WHY?

KATHRYN. Oh, Jeremy . . . I couldn't walk out on you with Mr. Ivorsen coming!

JEREMY. *(As she unbuttons coat, he re-buttons it, about two buttons behind.)* This is a fine time to turn loyal!

KATHRYN. But Jeremy—? I . . . I love you!

(CHARLIE re-enters, with martini for courage, stands near mantel, watching, a resigned and totally disinterested observer.)

JEREMY. Then go to a *hotel!*

KATHRYN. But what about Mr. Ivorsen?

JEREMY. *He* stays *here!*

TINA. *(Enters from kitchen with soup tureen, crosses down to table, on:)* Why, Mrs. Troy! We weren't expecting *you* back!

KATHRYN. Jeremy! What is that woman doing in my best dress?

JEREMY. Pretending to be you!

KATHRYN. What for?

TINA. *(With delight.)* Ten dollars an hour!

KATHRYN. Ten? This morning it was five—shouldn't you be declaring a dividend?

JEREMY. Kathryn, *Charlie* sent for Miss Winslow—

KATHRYN. And *you're* paying her?

JEREMY. But not for the same thing! . . . I mean—
Miss Winslow is an artist's model—

KATHRYN. (*As, unnoticed by anyone,* IVORSEN *enters
from bathroom.*) Oh, sure! Sure! And *I'm* the Princess of
Rumania—

IVORSEN. (*Booms delightedly.*) How do you *do!* (ALL
*freeze, horrified, staring Downstage, then slowly turn their
heads to follow him as he trots eagerly downstairs; at
bottom, he bows, clicks his heels, for:*) Your Highness!
(*Crosses to still-speechless* KATHRYN, *takes hand.*) My
name is Ivorsen. You can call me "Sven"! (*Kisses her
hand, then straightens, puzzled; positions are now, from
Downstage Right:* KATHRYN, IVORSEN, CHARLIE, JEREMY
and TINA, *still doggedly ladling out soup into bowls; to
CHARLIE:*) But what is a princess of royal blood doing in
New Jersey?

(CHARLIE *stares, then turns, passing the query to*
JEREMY.)

JEREMY. She has given up her throne for love.

IVORSEN. No kidding! . . . Love of whom?

JEREMY. (*"Gallantly" passes the hot potato back:*)
Charlie!

CHARLIE. (*With foreboding, crosses above* IVORSEN *to*
KATHRYN'S *side.*) Uh . . . Hi, there, Your Highness,
darling!

IVORSEN. But this is splendid! You know, Your Highness, I only met your intended this evening, but I can
guarantee you're getting a *prince.*

KATHRYN. (*As* CHARLIE *attempts to place his arm
across her shoulders.*) *Down,* Prince!

IVORSEN. Believe it or not—*I* know a little Rumanian—

TINA. What's his name?

IVORSEN. I mean, I understand the language.

KATHRYN. I *don't!*

CHARLIE. (*As* IVORSEN *reacts, covers with:*) That's *another* reason she gave up her throne—

TINA. (*Getting a desperate "Do something!" gesture from* JEREMY:) Well . . . I'll just go get another little old place setting—

IVORSEN. My dear, is there anything I can do to help?

TINA. Would you be an absolute darling and help me bring it in from the little old kitchen?

IVORSEN. Gladly, my dear! (*Starts off, remembers manners, fumbles bow at* KATHRYN, *exits after* TINA *into kitchen.*)

KATHRYN. (*Comes to* JEREMY, *removing her coat, as* CHARLIE *gets highbacked chair and carries it to Upstage Center of table.*) Have you two lost your *minds?* How long do you think you can *fool* him?

JEREMY. (*Taking her coat, etc.*) Don't desert me, darling. *Be* the princess until Ivorsen leaves, and then I'll explain everything—

KATHRYN. (*Submissive, but grim.*) Well, I'll jes' do ma li'l ol' *best!*

JEREMY. *Don't* play your *highness* with an accent—

KATHRYN. *She's* playing *me* with an accent—

CHARLIE. (*En route behind fireplace for more chairs.*) Only because you're not Spanish!

JEREMY. (*As* KATHRYN *goggles, takes her coat, etc., behind fireplace, on:*) Be good? Please?

(*Any response is forestalled by* TINA's *re-entrance with* IVORSEN *in her wake, carrying the place setting.*)

TINA. Why, thank you, *ever* so—*Mis-ter-I-vor-sen!*

IVORSEN. (*As* OTHERS *heed warning, goes to* KATHRYN; JEREMY *and* CHARLIE *meanwhile placing remainder of chairs at table.*) Your highness—if I may be so bold— What is your *given* name?

KATHRYN. (*As others freeze, listening, since they'll have to know it.*) *Ingeborg!* (JEREMY *and* CHARLIE *drop their chairs.*)

IVORSEN. A lovely name! Imagine: "Ingeborg Bickle!" (CHARLIE, *imagining, drains his drink; then, to* CHARLIE:) What do *you* think of it?

CHARLIE. I'm trying *not* to—

IVORSEN. You know—there's just one thing puzzles me about you and Ingeborg.

JEREMY. Just *one?*

IVORSEN. Where in the world did you two ever meet?

CHARLIE. Uh . . . that's a rather long, involved story—

KATHRYN. Naturally.

IVORSEN. I'd like to hear it.

TINA. (*Has placed setting on table, now forgets realities of things:*) Gee, so would I!

CHARLIE. (*Furious with her, tight-lipped:*) *I'd* rather hear where *you* met *Jeremy*—

KATHRYN. *So would I!*

JEREMY. Sir—! *I'd* rather hear how *you* met *your* wife.

IVORSEN. (*Reminiscently.*) It . . . It was funny, the way I met Audrey . . . (*As* OTHERS *wait, his smile slowly fades into rueful misery; then:*) Say—! *Is* there a royal family in Rumania?

(*Looks at* CHARLIE, *who looks at* JEREMY, *who looks at* TINA.)

TINA. Not any more. Ingeborg is the end of the line.

IVORSEN. (*To* KATHRYN, *solicitously.*) It's not easy being royalty these days!

KATHRYN. It's a lot easier than you imagine!

IVORSEN. I don't follow you, Ingeborg.

JEREMY. Good!

IVORSEN. And—come to think of it—"Ingeborg" isn't a *Rumanian* name—

CHARLIE. (*With super-patriotism.*) She's an *American,* now!

TINA. (*As usual, over-gilding the lily:*) Why, *she* even knows the *national anthem.* (*Bustles off toward kitchen, oblivious of fury on* CONSPIRATORS' *faces, pauses to suggest brightly, as she passes* KATHRYN:) Why dontcha sing it? (*Exits happily off to kitchen, as* KATHRYN *stands aghast, for:*)

IVORSEN. Oh, *sing* it, Your Highness!

KATHRYN. (*Steels herself; then, faces Downstage, hand going over heart, on:*) "Oh, say—" (CHARLIE'S *hand goes over his heart on:*) "can you—" (JEREMY'S *hand goes over his heart on:*) "see . . . !" (*Then, just as* IVORSEN *belatedly starts his hand over his heart:*) That's all I know.

IVORSEN. Five words?

CHARLIE. That's more than Christopher Columbus knew—

IVORSEN. (*Laughs, successfully sidetracked, offers* KATHRYN *his arm, leads her toward table, during:*) Your Highness—as laudable as your consort-to-be's job may be —doesn't it get under your skin having him work on other women?

KATHRYN. Oh— Only on the days they're in the *nude*, just a little!

CHARLIE. Uh. Darling, no one can be in the nude just a *little*—

IVORSEN. (*Not sidetracked this time.*) You work on your patients in the *nude?*

CHARLIE. Only at their request!

(TINA *enters from kitchen on his line, with large dinner gong, and strikes it;* OTHERS *all react violently, recover, as she hangs it at Right corner of mantel, comes down toward table.*)

JEREMY. Soup's getting cold! Let's eat!

(*As* IVORSEN *assists* KATHRYN *into second chair from Left,* JEREMY *and* CHARLIE, *at—respectively—Left and Right end-chairs, realize they'll be paired with wrong women, switch; as they get to ends,* TINA *gallantly assists a surprised* IVORSEN *into Center chair, then stands waiting for already-seated* JEREMY'S *help;* IVORSEN *notes this, clears throat loudly at* JEREMY; JEREMY *jumps up, sweetly pulls chair back for* TINA; *she starts to sit demurely at* IVORSEN'S *Right, and—as* IVORSEN *turns away—* JEREMY *shoves her violently down into place, then sits grimly at his own; as he puts napkin on lap,* CHARLIE *pulls table to himself, leaving* JEREMY *far from table;* JEREMY *pulls table back to himself, leaving* CHARLIE *ditto; as* CHARLIE *starts to pull it back,* IVORSEN *reaches across it to Downstage edge, stops it, pulls it back to himself;* JEREMY *and* CHARLIE *reluctantly hitch their chairs up to ends of table, and all* PARTICIPANTS *lift soup spoons, waiting for* IVORSEN *to begin.*)

IVORSEN. (*To* KATHRYN, *his spoon still poised.*) Snowy weather always gives me an appetite. It's really *piling up* out there.

KATHRYN. Out *there?*

JEREMY. Come on, let's eat.

(ALL *bend, sip spoonful of soup; beat;* ALL *but* TINA *slowly rise, faces mingling horror and incredulity;* TINA *continues to eat,* ALL *of them watching her with amazement for about three sips; then:*)

IVORSEN. My dear . . . such an unusual flavor . . . what kind of soup *is* this?

TINA. (*Pleased.*) Cream of lettuce! Do you like it? It's my own recipe: Lettuce leaves, milk, a teaspoon of ginger, and just a little flour!

CHARLIE. (*Idly paddling tip of spoon in his bowl.*) I think the little flower has wilted—

IVORSEN. But honestly, Kathryn, this is simply delicious. So very original. I can't imagine what the main course will be.

TINA. It's going to be a surprise—

CHARLIE. Amen!

JEREMY. Let me pour the wine. There's nothing so warming as a glass of wine on a cold winter's night. (*Pours for each as they extend goblets.*) Your Highness?

KATHRYN. Yes. Quickly. For the love of heaven!

CHARLIE. This is the night for wine, all right. There must be two feet of snow on the lawn, and more on the way.

IVORSEN. (*Thoughtfully, just as* JEREMY *finishes pouring.*) You know— I dread the thought of going back to New York tonight— (OTHERS *freeze, looking at one another, for one beat; then they bend forward in unison and begin diligently sipping their soup;* IVORSEN *thinks they've missed the hint, begins to amplify:*) I mean—it's going to be a long, wearisome drive for me . . . (*Sip, sip, sip.*) out in the cold air . . . (*Sip, sip, sip.*) bad visibility . . . (*Sip, sip, sip.*) slippery roads . . . !

JEREMY. (*Hears the edge in his voice, has to raise his head to speak.*) Uh . . . you know, Mister Ivorsen— (OTHERS *lift faces apprehensively, pleadingly; he says, lamely:*) you've hardly touched your soup! (*Dives to join* OTHERS *in united sip, sip, sip.*)

IVORSEN. (*Nettled, booms:*) What I *meant* was—I don't suppose you could put me up for the night? (*The threat is in the open, now;* OTHERS' *heads all come up, now.*)

JEREMY. You mean—*here*, sir?

IVORSEN. Of course, here! Wouldn't be too much trouble, would it?

JEREMY. Well—the thing is—Charlie and Ingeborg are using the guest room—

KATHRYN. That's what you think!

CHARLIE. Jeremy means the guest *facilities*. I'm taking the sofa—

KATHRYN. —and I'm taking the room.

IVORSEN. Couldn't I *share* the guest room?

KATHRYN. *Mis*-ter *Ivorsen!*

IVORSEN. I mean with *Charlie?*

JEREMY. And put the princess on the sofa?

IVORSEN. Good heavens, I didn't think! I apologize, Your Highness!

KATHRYN. Oh— Very well. I accept your apology. It was nothing.

JEREMY. Uh. Sir. She doesn't mean your *apology* was nothing—

KATHRYN. Oh! No! What you said *before* was nothing—

CHARLIE. Your apology was really *something!*

IVORSEN. Aw, it was nothing!

TINA. (*Folds arms meticulously as she announces, with some acerbity:*) Maybe we should take a vote! (ALL *look her way, death in all but* IVORSEN'S *gaze; she reacts.*) I'll just—get the plates! (*Rises hastily, gathering soup bowls and spoons.*)

KATHRYN. (*Doing same.*) I'll *help* you.

JEREMY. (*Doesn't dare let those two be alone in kitchen.*) So will I.

(*The three exit,* TINA *pursued by* KATHRYN *pursued by* JEREMY.)

IVORSEN. Imagine a princess helping with the plates! I do wish you'd tell me where you met this paragon.

CHARLIE. (*Has had time to cook a story up, now, so says smoothly:*) Ingeborg was a patient of mine. Fell off her polo pony and got a *mallet* in the teeth!

IVORSEN. But she has *beautiful* teeth.

CHARLIE. Caps. Best work I ever did!

KATHRYN. (*Re-enters, comes down to place on tag of his line, sing-songing:*) *I* just got a look at the *en*-tree—

IVORSEN. (*As she sits to his Left again.*) I'll bet it's really something, eh?

KATHRYN. (*As a glassy-eyed* JEREMY *enters and regains his chair.*) Well, *I've* never seen anything like it!

(*Bares her teeth in a somewhat vicious smile at* JEREMY,

then reacts as IVORSEN *bends head to peer right in
her mouth, and gives "Okay!" high sign with thumb-
and-forefinger circle to* CHARLIE; *she turns a bewildered look at Charlie, who avoids her eyes to sip
his wine, just as* TINA *enters with a tray of what
appears to be individual pieces of cordwood on separate plates; she sets tray down on coffeetable, announcing:*)

TINA. Surprise, surprise, sur-prise!

IVORSEN. (*Craning to see, uneasily.*) Kathryn—what
are those things?

TINA. (*Handing plates to* JEREMY, *who passes all but
the last one down table, keeping that for himself.*) It's
steak! My own recipe. I call it "Chicken in the Wood"!
Of course, there's no *chicken* in it . . ..

CHARLIE. (*Eyeing his portion dubiously.*) How about
wood?

TINA. Silly! That's because they're shaped like little
old logs! See, the chicken part is eggs. You roll up three
fresh eggs in each steak, fasten it together with tooth-
picks, seal the ends of the tubes with slices of lemon, then
bake in a slow oven for two hours—-

CHARLIE. Well . . . *steak*-and-*eggs* doesn't sound
bad . . .

IVORSEN. Not bad at all . . . As a matter of fact, I
can't wait. (*Starts to cut his; there comes an audible
CRUNCH; tries again; the CRUNCH is heard again;
sets down knife, asks unhappily:*) What was that?

TINA. (*Taking final plate from tray.*) Why, the *eggs*,
silly! (*Starts for her place.*)

IVORSEN. (*Not quite in tears.*) You mean—they're in
the *shells?*

TINA. Well, you *have* to do it that way. (*With descrip-
tive gestures.*) The other way, everything just *runs* all
over. (*Sits down demurely, on:*) *This* way, *every one* is
nicely *trapped!*

CHARLIE. (*Hoists wine glass.*) I'll drink to *that!*

KATHRYN. I'll join you! (*They drink, as:*)

JEREMY. (*To* TINA, *with tight jaw and taut suspicion.*) Why, Kathryn, *darling*, what is that on *your* plate—?

TINA. A ham sandwich. I only planned dinner for four.

OTHERS. (*Lift and thrust plates toward her in unison, on:*) *Here!* Take *mine!*

TINA. Oh, but I don't mind. Really I don't.

KATHRYN. (*Stands, imperiously.*) As Royal High Princess of Rumania— (*Then breaks dignity, grabs plate on:*) gimme that sandwich! (*Sits and starts to tear into sandwich; PHONE rings;* TINA *rises.*) I'll get it—! (TINA *sits as* KATHRYN, *taking plate with her, goes to phone.*) Hello? . . .

IVORSEN. Imagine that—she answered the phone!

CHARLIE. She even ties her own tennis shoes!

KATHRYN. (*On phone, just as* IVORSEN *just slightly suspects* CHARLIE'S *reply.*) Just a moment, please . . . (*Thrusts phone toward* TINA.) It's for you, *Kathryn*—

TINA. (*To* IVORSEN, *nervously polite, distracting him from* CHARLIE.) 'Scuse me! (*Takes phone gingerly from icy-miened* KATHRYN, *who sits and begins making voracious inroads on ham sandwich, during:*) Hello? . . . Oh, *hi*, Pop! . . . (*Leans confidentially toward* IVORSEN.) It's my father . . . (*Adds, she thinks, explanatorily:*) *Mister Troy!* . . .

IVORSEN. (*Reacts, turns back to* JEREMY, *who quickly hides own reaction, on:*) *Her* father's name is Troy?

JEREMY. He—he had it changed, for tax purposes—

IVORSEN. How did *that* help?

CHARLIE. It didn't.

TINA. (*Back to group, on phone:*) Honestly, Pop, Jeremy is being a perfect gentleman—

JEREMY. (*Desperately, as* IVORSEN *reacts.*) Uh, Charlie—! When is Ingeborg's abdication final?

CHARLIE. Yesterday!

JEREMY. Must have been a terrible blow to her supporters.

CHARLIE. Shook the kingdom to its foundation!

IVORSEN. (*To quiet their loudness so* TINA *can hear on phone.*) Gentlemen—gentlemen! Ssssh!

(*Gestures toward* TINA; *silence falls, so* ALL *hear.*)

TINA. (*Loudly.*) Well, of *course* I've got my clothes on! (*Freezes, feeling all eyes on her, hangs up phone, whirls.*) Well . . . I *have!* (ALL *still stare; so, almost in tears:*) I'll go see about dessert!

(*As she flees to safety of kitchen,* JEREMY *and* CHARLIE *drain wine glasses,* KATHRYN *nonchalantly finishes ham sandwich, and* IVORSEN *rises, ominously, dropping his napkin onto table.*)

IVORSEN. What time is it getting to be? (*Before anyone can tell him, suddenly goes wide-eyed, pushes back chair, starts looking about, moving tigerishly to and fro, on:*) Good heavens! Where is it? I don't see it—help me find it—

JEREMY. (*Jumps up, looking wildly about, for about two beats; then stops.*) What is it we're *looking* for, sir?

IVORSEN. You *have* a TV set, don't you?

JEREMY. Oh! Yes, sir. Downstairs in our recreation room, but— (*As* IVORSEN *hurries in indicated direction.*) don't you want to wait for dessert, sir?

IVORSEN. (*At Left archway, as* JEREMY *comes up to him.*) First things first, Jeremy! . . . *Perry Mason* is on! (*Remembers himself to others.*) Your Highness . . . Doctor Bickle . . . ! (*Exits behind fireplace,* JEREMY *trailing haplessly after him.*)

KATHRYN. "*Doctor*" Bickle?

CHARLIE. (*Rises, starts moving table kitchenward.*) I'll just take this out to the woodshed—

KATHRYN. Charlie. (*He stops, almost at Right archway, turns.*) *What* is going *on* around here, *anyhow?*

CHARLIE. If you'd stuck around, this morning, you'd know. No. wait, that's not fair. If you'd stuck around, this morning, none of this *would* be going on. Where the heck have you *been*, anyhow?

KATHRYN. Walking. Wandering, really. Trying to put the pieces of my broken life back together. Wading along through the snow, downtown, staring through my tears into all the pretty windows—like Stella Dallas!

CHARLIE. All this time?

(He and KATHRYN automatically begin putting chairs back in their proper places, during rest of their lines together.)

KATHRYN. All this time. I *couldn't* come back *too* soon, after that exit! Oh, walking out in a rage is a grand feeling at first, as you shout your goodbyes and slam the door in a blaze of righteousness! Then you start to think: "Where am I going? What am I going to do? How far can I get on eighteen dollars and a pack of Dentyne?" A block from the house, you stop and look back, hoping you'll see him running after you. But he isn't. So you walk a bit slower. And still he doesn't come. And there you are, shivering out in the freezing wind, while he remains in the nice warm house. *Your* house. But a farewell is a farewell, so you keep walking, proud and brave and aloof, courageously facing the future alone. This phase lasts about fifteen minutes. Meantime, your feet are starting to hurt, the snow is coming down harder, it's getting dark out, all your Kleenex is gone, and you suddenly remember that next Monday night is your turn to have the bridge club! The next thing you know, you're hailing a cab, urging the driver to run the red lights, leaping out at your front walk, jamming a bill into the driver's hand and telling him to keep the change, and then galloping up your front stairs with only one thought in mind: "Can I parlay my husband's remorse into a new living-room set?" *(Sits on sofa, folds arms, leans back, lifts legs onto coffee table and crosses ankles, resignedly, on:)* I should be ashamed of myself.

CHARLIE. Don't be. You've just restored my lack of confidence in human nature!

(*Exits to kitchen with table, passing* TINA *on way out, with tray of individual slices of brownish-grey pie on separate saucers.*)

TINA. I think I spoiled the dessert.

KATHRYN. (*Turns head, views servings on tray.*) How can you tell?

CHARLIE. (*Enters from kitchen, espies dessert.*) Hey, that actually looks good! What kind of pie *is* it?

TINA. Black-Eyed Pea Pie.

CHARLIE. Well— It still *looks* good . . .

JEREMY. (*Enters via Left archway, heads directly for* KATHRYN.) Now, darling, if you'll just let me explain— You see, Mr. Ivorsen was coming, and—

KATHRYN. (*Rises, shaking her head in angry bemusement, on:*) Jeremy, I can't *stand* that man! How have you been able to manage seven years' worth?

CHARLIE. Kathryn, a man can do anything with the right woman to inspire him!

KATHRYN. Now, don't start *that* again! Jeremy, once and for all—who do you love?

JEREMY. You, of course! There's never been anyone else for me.

KATHRYN. What about— (*Looks at* TINA, *controls herself, reduces the epithet to:*) Betty Crocker?

CHARLIE. Don't be an idiot. The way to a man's heart is through his *stomach*.

KATHRYN. You know, that's almost *convincing?*

JEREMY. Kathy—!

TINA. Charlie, was that a crack—?

CHARLIE. You mean you *really* cook like that—?

JEREMY. If you two would be *quiet* a moment—

KATHRYN. It'll take more than a moment to—

(ALL *have been speaking loudly and furiously, and now abruptly freeze and fall silent as* IVORSEN *enters un-*

expectedly through Left archway; he goes to TINA, *takes piece of pie and fork from tray, turns, starts for archway, senses their combined gazes, turns in archway, and:*)

IVORSEN. Commercial. (*Exits.*)

JEREMY. (*Rushes to* KATHRYN, *takes her hands.*) Darling, please listen! There may not be another chance! Tina *is* an artist's model, and Charlie *did* send for her.

KATHRYN. Then—what *were* you apologizing for, this morning?

JEREMY. (*Beat; then, since it's too far gone for evasions, says flatly.*) I never got a law degree.

KATHRYN. You never—? Jeremy! You did, too—I saw you get it!—I was there.

JEREMY. It was a fake. A forgery!

KATHRYN. Forgery? But—why? Why would you forge a law degree?

JEREMY. Because I knew you were crazy about lawyers— (*When she can only stand and gape:*) You *said* so.

KATHRYN. (*Wonderingly, softly.*) Jeremy. You dope. What did *you* say to *me*, just *before* that?

JEREMY. (*At sea.*) That—I was in law school—but—?

KATHRYN. Darling. You mean— Jeremy, don't you get it, *yet?* If you'd said medical school, I'd have been dotty about doctors. If you'd been in engineering, I'd have been buggy about bridges.

JEREMY. Kathy! You were wild about *me?*

KATHRYN. And still am, you crazy, mixed-up Machiavelli! When I think of it—! All these years—no degree —and— (*A whoop of amusement.*) the governor shook your hand! (*Sobers, as she realizes:*) No *wonder* you fainted when you saw Charlie. (*Then, very tenderly, indeed:*) Oh, Jeremy . . . darling . . . I love you.

TINA. Gee, this is exciting.

(KATHRYN *and* JEREMY *suddenly remember* CHARLIE *and* TINA.)

KATHRYN. Would you two—? No, never mind! Jeremy, come with me into the kitchen where we can be alone. (*She and* JEREMY *exit, she pulling him by the hand.*)

TINA. (*Puzzled, sets tray of pie on coffee table, on:*) Can't they be alone in the living room?

CHARLIE. (*Sitting at Right end of sofa.*) Only between commercials. (*As* TINA *crosses behind sofa to draped windows.*) Can you imagine a guy trying a dumb stunt like that?

TINA. (*Back to him, about to pull drapes open, looks over shoulder for:*) Oh, I wouldn't talk if I were you— *talent scout! (Turns away as he reacts, pulls drapes, then looks back at him.*) "Lemme see your legs!" (*Her mimicry is mocking, and he winces.*)

CHARLIE. (*Stung, says defensively:*) That was sincere. As an artist, I think very highly of those legs. As a matter of fact, I intend painting them, soon as I get the chance.

TINA. (*A nod toward the impressionistic horror.*) Not if they end up looking like *that* thing over the *fireplace.*

CHARLIE. I can be realistic when I want to be.

TINA. (*Looks at him, and we can feel the electricity on:*) So can I . . . (*As if abruptly indifferent, she looks out window, and:*) Isn't the view lovely out there tonight?

CHARLIE. (*He got his cue, and is not muffing it; she is within reach, and he pulls her back over sofa-arm onto his lap, gently and deftly, on:*) Yeah. Nothing beats moonrise over the Doeskin Tissue Factory! (*He kisses her, she kisses back, and while they are doing a superb job of it,* IVORSEN *enters through Left archway, sees them, reacts, and ducks back, peering popeyed around edge of mantel;* TINA *begins to shake, then to giggle, then leans back and laughs.*) Well, *I* enjoyed it, too, but it wasn't *that* much fun . . . *Was* it?

TINA. I'm sorry. I was just picturing Jeremy's face.

CHARLIE. Well, you were kissing *mine!*

TINA. I mean what his face would look like if he could see us now!

CHARLIE. (*They* BOTH *laugh; then:*) Hey, can you

picture old *Ivorsen's* face if *he* could see us now? (BOTH *roar even louder, as* IVORSEN *reacts with increased shock.*) Say, what's the final set-up on this overnight business, anyway? If Ivorsen's staying, we've got to make sure who's sleeping where.

TINA. That's *right!* If I'm not careful, *I* may end up spending the night with *Jeremy.* There's a ghastly thought.

(BOTH *whoop again; then:*)

CHARLIE. But old Ivorsen's so hipped on this devoted-little-wife act of yours that he may insist on it!

TINA. (*Starts to rise;* IVORSEN, *panic-stricken, exits, fast, to cellar.*) Well, no matter *who* I'm sleeping with to-night, I'd better tell my father!

(CHARLIE *goes to nod, then reacts, stares after her as she goes toward telephone;* KATHRYN *and* JEREMY *enter from kitchen.*)

CHARLIE. (*Sees them, and that they are obviously on good terms.*) Well? Are you convinced yet?

KATHRYN. (*Reluctant to admit her conviction so quickly.*) Jeremy's got me *darn near* convinced . . . (*Then, enjoying the role of fellow-conspirator:*) We even figured out who can sleep where.

CHARLIE. (*Rises delightedly.*) Then the pajama party's on? Good! Now, if Tina can only convince her father— (*Starts toward desk, where* TINA *is dialing phone.*)

JEREMY. Say, Ivorsen's due back up here any time, now. You'd better use the extension up in our bedroom, Tina—

TINA. (*Hangs up, starts for stairs.*) That's probably a good idea!

CHARLIE. (*Following.*) I'll come along and give you moral support, honey!

JEREMY. *Honey?*

CHARLIE. (*As* TINA *enters bedroom.*) I, too; have my moments! (*Exits after her, shuts door.*)

JEREMY. (*Laughs; turns to see* KATHRYN *picking up pie, hors d'oeuvre, etc.*) Hey, don't get too domestic, honey. You're a princess, remember?

KATHRYN. I used to clean up af'er the king.

JEREMY. (*Goes to her.*) Aw, honey— I love you— (BOTH *forget clean-up, sit side-by-side on sofa.*)

KATHRYN. Too bad Mr. Ivorsen's wife is in Florida. On a cold night like this, nothing beats a warm spouse under the blankets.

JEREMY. I'll bet *Mrs.* Ivorsen's not cold, tonight! She's probably reclining on warm, moonlit sands, giving come-hither glances to the nearest lifeguard!

KATHRYN. Jeremy, shame on you!

JEREMY. Shame on Mrs. Ivorsen!

(BOTH *start to chuckle; then stop as they hear a loud clearing of a throat;* IVORSEN *appears in Left archway, still hidden from them, and clears throat a second time; they shift a bit apart; then he enters, sees them, and reacts in bewilderment, looking around for couple he had expected to find on the sofa.*)

KATHRYN. (*Interested by his furtive manner.*) Is there anything wrong—?

IVORSEN. (*Almost in a whisper:*) Are you two alone?

JEREMY. Well—we *were* . . .

(KATHRYN *giggles.*)

IVORSEN. This is no laughing matter, Your Highness! I'm afraid I am the bearer of—tragic tidings.

KATHRYN. Why . . . Mr. Ivorsen . . . you seem troubled—

IVORSEN. I am. Deeply. (*Moves somberly to sofa, sits between* TWOSOME; *then, mournfully:*) Recently—very recently—certain facts have come into my possession . . .

JEREMY. What facts, sir?

IVORSEN. Facts that may shatter a marriage I had imagined to be—perfect. (*He's hunched sadly forward;* JEREMY *and* KATHRYN *exchange a knowing—well, they think they know—look, over his back; then:*)

JEREMY. What—what did it, sir?

KATHRYN. Was it moonlit nights—?

JEREMY. Warm sands—?

IVORSEN. I—I think it was a soft sofa.

JEREMY. But couldn't you be mistaken, sir? Is there any chance that—?

IVORSEN. I overheard them talking.

KATHRYN. You may have misunderstood.

IVORSEN. Their words were all too *crimsonly* clear.

KATHRYN. Oh, how terrible for you!

IVORSEN. A wife I'd supposed gentle, innocent and loyal, and a man I had come to think of as a friend . . .

JEREMY. A loving wife—

KATHRYN. —a trusted friend . . .

IVORSEN. The old, old story!

KATHRYN. What did you do?

IVORSEN. (*Rises, ashamed, moves toward stairs, his back toward sofa.*) Nothing! Oh, it was cowardly of me, I admit, but I was too shaken to think clearly. Instead of announcing my presence, I turned and fled.

JEREMY. I think—if I'd have been in your position, sir—I'd have spoken.

IVORSEN. (*Turns, somewhat puzzled by reaction he's getting from* TWOSOME.) Well, naturally! But it wasn't really my place to do so.

KATHRYN. But—Mr. Ivorsen—who had a *better* right?

JEREMY. (*Stands, husky-voiced with sympathetic fury.*) Who's the man, sir? Have I met him?

IVORSEN. Of course you have! It's—Charlie. Your friend, Charlie!

KATHRYN. (*Rises, incredulous.*) Charlie Bickle from the university?

JEREMY. But sir, I didn't know he'd even *met* your wife!

IVORSEN. (*Turns on them with a bull-roar of reaction:*) *My* wife? Are you out of your mind? I'm talking about *your* wife, on this very sofa, not fifteen minutes ago!

(*The revelation is too much for* JEREMY *and* KATHRYN, *who drop down laughing uproariously onto sofa again.*)

KATHRYN. Is *that* all?

IVORSEN. All? Isn't that enough? Your fiance—and your wife! . . . Jeremy—Ingeborg! They were planning on whom they were going to—*sleep* with— They *didn't* exactly say with one another, but they sure eliminated everybody *else*. (*Is by now standing behind sofa, looking thunderstruck at the* TWOSOME, *who can scarcely control their impulse to laugh aloud.*) Say! Where *are* they all this time?

JEREMY. (*Controls himself to blurt:*) Oh, they're just upstairs in the *bedroom*— (*This shatters* KATHRYN'S *control, and she whoops.*) But only to make a phone call!

IVORSEN. (*Gestures toward phone on desk.*) And what do you call *that* instrument?

KATHRYN. (*Controls herself to blurt:*) They just didn't want to be *disturbed*— (JEREMY *now whoops, and she joins him, helplessly.*)

IVORSEN. And apparently neither do the two of you! Hasn't the enormity of the situation gotten through to you?

JEREMY. (*Stands, holding his twitching smile-muscles in check.*) Of course it has. And we're both h-highly indignant—

KATHRYN. (*Stands staunchly at his side, fighting her own spastic twitches.*) Yes. Highly.

IVORSEN. Well, you could've fooled *me*.

(*The jig is nearly up;* JEREMY *gets real control, goes to* IVORSEN, *followed a moment later by a semi-controlled* KATHRYN, *during:*)

JEREMY. It's just that—I'd rather not have a scene while you're our guest, sir. Tomorrow morning, when the others have gone—I will have a talk with Kathryn.

KATHRYN. And I will have a talk with Charles. This is the sort of thing best discussed only by the parties involved.

IVORSEN. I understand. I misjudged you both. But— now that you know—what possible sleeping arrangements can we make?

JEREMY. Well, I thought—Kathryn and Ingeborg in the guest room, you and Charlie in the main bedroom, and me on the sofa—

IVORSEN. Admirable! In that way, I can watch *Charlie* all night, you—Ingeborg—can watch *Kathryn* all night, and you—Jeremy—uh—?

JEREMY. *I* can watch *television* all night!

IVORSEN. That's it, son. Keep up a brave front. (*Claps* JEREMY *on shoulder, just as* TINA *and* CHARLIE *emerge from bedroom; in doorway,* TINA *stops* CHARLIE *to wipe lipstick from his face, before they start downstairs.*) Did you see *that?*

JEREMY. I'm fighting hard for self-control, sir!

IVORSEN. Good man! (*Then, louder-voiced for benefit of new arrivals at foot of stairs.*) Well—it's getting late. Guess I'll be turning in. (*Walks past a smiling* TINA *and* CHARLIE *to stairs; their smiles fade as they pivot, slowly, watching his icy gaze in surprise.*) I'll be seeing you upstairs, young man . . . (*Ascends, turns at bedroom door for:*) shortly! (*Exits.*)

CHARLIE. What's with *him?*

JEREMY. Never mind him. What's with Tina?

TINA. Pop said no. If I'm not home in twenty minutes he's going to send the vice squad after me!

CHARLIE. (*Heading Upstage for coats.*) I'll have to drive her home.

KATHRYN. But what'll we tell Mr. Ivorsen in the morning?

CHARLIE. (*During next lines, helps* TINA *into coat,*

dons an overcoat himself.) We've got that all figured out:
I take Tina home, now, and come back here myself.
When Ivorsen gets up in the morning, we'll tell him she's
gone out shopping.

TINA. And once it's daylight, that's what I *will* do,
and come here—

JEREMY. With the groceries—of course! I couldn't have
come up with a better scheme myself.

CHARLIE. Tina, you have just been paid the highest
possible compliment.

KATHRYN. It's sure to work.

CHARLIE. Unless old Ivorsen sneaks a peek into the
guest room.

KATHRYN. It has a strong bolt and no keyhole.

TINA. Oh, Kathryn—I'll return your dress tomorrow,
okay? I don't have time to change now.

KATHRYN. That'll be fine, Tina. Thanks for your help.

JEREMY. (*Recognizing garment just as they get to
door.*) Hey, Charlie—you can't wear Mr. Ivorsen's *overcoat!*

CHARLIE. (*As* TINA *exits, lifts keys from pocket, twirls
them on:*) Why not? I'm using his *car.* (*Exits after* TINA;
front door closes.)

KATHRYN. (*Returns to items on coffee table, starts to
clear them.*) I hope that car has snow tires!

JEREMY. Want a hand doing the dishes, honey?

KATHRYN. No, I'm just going to stack everything in
the sink. I've had a very tiring day! (*Hands things to
him.*)

JEREMY. (*Starts for kitchen as she starts for window
seat.*) Haven't we all! Well, maybe tomorrow will be
better. (*Exits.*)

KATHRYN. (*Taking bedding from inside window seat.*)
It'd *have* to be. (*Starts making up sofa;* JEREMY *re-
enters, starts to help her.*)

JEREMY. You know something, Kathy—this will be our
first night apart since we've been married—

KATHRYN. Jeremy Troy, if you're thinking **what** I

think you're thinking, I think you'd better think *again*
. . . Besides, I know you better than you imagine: You're
not yearning for me, you're yearning for a comfortable
place to sleep. (*Starts for stairs.*)

JEREMY. Aw, honey—!

KATHRYN. (*En route upstairs.*) And don't try creeping
upstairs later. For your own good, I'm going to shoot that
bolt.

JEREMY. But I'm not sleepy yet . . .

KATHRYN. (*At head of stairs.*) Well, I am. Why don't
you go down and watch a late movie? That always makes
you start to doze off.

JEREMY. Guess I might as well. 'Night, honey.

KATHRYN. Good night, Darling.

(KATHRYN *blows him a kiss, exits into guest room;*
JEREMY *sighs, goes to Left archway, flicks wall
switch that douses all LIGHTS; we see a flicker of
LIGHT momentarily as he exits to cellar; two beats;
then we see a brief flood of STREETLAMP-LIGHT
in Upstage passageway, and a pair of silhouettes,
then blackness, and hear:*)

CHARLIE. All clear!

(*LIGHTS come up full;* CHARLIE, *shoeless, tie askew,
minus both overcoat and suit jacket, tiptoes into
room, shivering, followed by* TINA, *shoulders draped
in his suit jacket, her dress sodden and in shreds;
she goes to phone, sneezes, starts to dial.*)

TINA. I feel just *awful* about Kathryn's lovely dress!

CHARLIE. Don't worry. All you have to do is let Jeremy
off the hook for your fee, and he can buy her a *new* dress.

TINA. How are you going to pay him for the tuxedo?

CHARLIE. I'll swap him a painting for it—

TINA. (*Sneezes again.*) I think I'm catching cold.

CHARLIE. You'd better get out of those wet things and
into a hot shower.

TINA. But I've got to talk to my father.

CHARLIE. (*Takes phone from her.*) I'll talk to him. You go take that shower.

TINA. Maybe I'd better. (*Hangs his suit jacket on newel post, starts tiptoeing upstairs, pauses to remove her shoes, then tiptoes rest of way up, crosses balcony, exits into bathroom and shuts door, during:*)

CHARLIE. (*On phone.*) Hello, Mr. Winslow? . . . This is Charles Bickle . . . I was just bringing your daughter home and we ran into a little trouble . . . You know that excavation at the corner of Pinecrest and Ridge? . . . Well, I just filled it with a Mercedes-Benz! . . . No, soft as a feather, really. We just sank down into ten feet of snow . . . Yes, she's fine, sir. Just a little wet, is all. But I'm afraid that car is there till the spring thaw . . . Well, I don't know exactly *when* she'll be home *now* . . . Everyone here's gone to bed . . . Listen, sir—why don't *you* come by for her—? . . . Yes, I *know* it's a rotten night, I was just *out* in it! . . . I see . . . Okay, sir, I'll tell her . . . Nice talking to you, too, sir . . . Don't mention it . . . 'Bye.

(*Hangs up, grins happily, grabs suit jacket as he trots upstairs and raps at bathroom door;* TINA, *without her glasses, walks out wrapped in only a towel, peers myopically into his face.*)

TINA. Who is it?

CHARLIE. It's *me*. Put your glasses on. (*She does so.*) Your father says you can stay.

TINA. How'd you work *that?*

CHARLIE. I offered to let *him* get dressed and come burrowing through the snowdrifts for you, and all at once he decided I had an honest voice, and said you could stay.

TINA. Why didn't *I* think of that? (*Pecks him on the lips.*) I'll be out of here in a jiffy.

CHARLIE. I'm too tired to take a shower. Just give me

that towel and I'll dry off before I hit the sack. (TINA *looks down at towel, then turns and pads into bathroom, returns with another towel, hands it to him, without comment.*) Thanks, hon. Good night. (*Another brief kiss.*)

TINA. Good night, Charlie . . . see you in the morning. (*Exits into bathroom, shuts door;* CHARLIE *moves to door of main bedroom, cracks it open, winces as loud SNORES are heard, squares his shoulders manfully, enters, shuts door;* JEREMY *emerges from cellar through Left archway, sees lights are on, puzzledly turns them OFF, then ON again, shrugs, looks at made-up sofa, frowns, pats stomach ruminatively, then exits into kitchen; beat;* TINA, *still only in towel, emerges from bathroom, tries guest-room door, finds it locked, raps, listens at it, then comes slowly downstairs.*) Jeremy . . . ? Kathryn . . . ? Hey . . . anybody—? (*Looks at sofa, shrugs.*) Well—you must be for me!

(*Turns out LIGHTS at Left archway, does not notice kitchen light is still on, crosses to sofa in pale MOONLIGHT now coming through window, lies down, turns over, goes to sleep; three beats; then* KATHRYN *appears, silhouetted against guest room doorway in nightgown, comes over to railing of balcony for:*)

KATHRYN. Jeremy . . . ? Darling, was that you at my door? . . . Aw, the poor darling!

(*Tiptoes back into guest room, shuts door; beat; then kitchen LIGHT goes out, and* JEREMY *steps into just-visibility in moonlight, looking about in puzzlement at the now-dark room he'd left lighted.*)

JEREMY. What the hell—?

(*Too tired to solve mystery, he undresses down to his shorts in front of window, draws drapes; Stage goes completely BLACK; two beats; then* TINA *screams, loudly and repeatedly; an instant later, silhouettes of* CHARLIE *and* KATHRYN *are seen at respective doorways,* CHARLIE *finds upstairs light switch, and LIGHTS come up full;* JEREMY *and* TINA *are standing on sofa, stunned, wrapped in same sheet;* KATHRYN *groans, falls into* CHARLIE'S *arms, sobbing;* IVORSEN *emerges in his underwear, see all four "properly paired," beams, exits.*)

CURTAIN

ACT THREE

The following morning, about 7:30 a.m. The room is slightly dim because the drapes are still drawn; when they are opened, brightness will come up full to match the opening of Act One. TINA *is asleep on the sofa, wrapped in a sheet, her legs exposed and toward the window.* JEREMY'S *clothes are no longer where he placed them when undressing. A moment after Curtain-rise,* CHARLIE *enters from bedroom, dressed as at the start of Act One; we hear* IVORSEN *snoring while the door is open.* CHARLIE, *bleary-eyed, starts for bathroom, looks down and sees* TINA; *he almost greets her cheerily, then remembers and scowls; he suddenly reacts to her legs, rushes back into bedroom, emerges with sketch pad and charcoal, dashes down to Right end of sofa, opens drapes, starts to sketch her legs; she has reacted to LIGHT, stirs, moves legs; gently, he places them back where they were, continues sketching;* KATHRYN *enters in robe from guest room, tries bathroom door; it is locked; she comes to rail, looks down.*

KATHRYN. Good morning, Doctor Bickle.
CHARLIE. (*Doggedly sketching.*) Your Highness.
KATHRYN. Apparently you slept as badly as I did.
CHARLIE. Probably worse. Ivorsen snores.
KATHRYN. He's still in bed?
CHARLIE. I didn't have the heart to kick him out.
KATHRYN. Then Jeremy must be the one monopolizing the bathroom. In which case— (*Knocks loudly on bathroom door, but speaks only in loud whisper:*) Hurry up in there! *Other* people have to brush their teeth!

(*Door opens, and a hunched figure emerges; it is* JEREMY,

80

tangle-haired, clothing rumpled, spine bent until he walks like an ambulant question-mark.)

JEREMY. Sorry to keep you waiting. I had trouble getting out of the tub.

CHARLIE. I take it you want us to believe you spent all of last night lying in the bathtub?

KATHRYN. As if he wasn't in enough hot water already!

(*Exits into bathroom;* JEREMY *painfully descends stairs, stumbles down last few, awakening* TINA, *who does not yet see* CHARLIE.)

TINA. Good morning!

CHARLIE. Good morning!

TINA. (*Turns head, sees him, sits up quickly, wrapping legs in sheet.*) Unless you two gentlemen want me to spend the rest of my life on this sofa, would one of you be so kind as to get me my clothes?

CHARLIE. Where are they?

TINA. In the closet in Mr. Ivorsen's room. I was wearing a yellow—

CHARLIE. *I* remember from yesterday! I'll get them. (*Ignoring* JEREMY, *goes upstairs, exits into bedroom; when he returns with her dress and shoes, he will be minus sketching gear.*)

TINA. He remembers. That's supposed to be a good sign a man likes you . . . when he notices what you're wearing . . . (*Buries face in hands, starts to sob.*)

KATHRYN. (*Enters from bathroom, waving the ruined gown.*) I hope that's *remorse* you're expressing down there. *Look* at this gown! It's ruined—what did you do, take a bath in it?

JEREMY. Not while *I* was in the tub, honey . . .

KATHRYN. I wouldn't put it past you! (*Exits into guest room, slams door.*)

TINA. (*Watching his slow, painful progress toward*

sofa.) I'm sorry you're all doubled up like that, Jeremy. I feel personally responsible. I should have given you the sofa and slept in the tub myself.

JEREMY. Don't mention it, Tina . . . You won the toss fair and square . . . I wonder if some old cathedral in New Jersey can use a bell-ringer?

TINA. (*Secures sheet with tuck, gets up, assists him toward sofa.*) Here, Jeremy, let me help you!

JEREMY. It's all right. I can manage. A few years' therapy at Johns Hopkins and I'll be almost like new. (*Sits with suppressed squeal of pain on sofa.*)

TINA. There must be something I can do to help—

JEREMY. (*Woefully, chin almost on knees, meaning what he says:*) Have me destroyed.

TINA. (*Bustles to a point above him, behind sofa.*) Listen, they taught us something helpful in modeling school— (*Gets her arms under his, around his chest.*) Models get stiff all the time from holding long poses. They showed us how to come unkinked. Now . . . try to relax . . .

JEREMY. (*Feet off floor, gnarled as an ancient oak.*) I *am* relaxed—

IVORSEN. (*Enters cheerily from bedroom, in tux, minus tie and jacket.*) Good mor-ning! And how are the little lovebirds?

TINA. (*Grimly, clutching* JEREMY, *reverts to southern drawl.*) Oh, jes' billin' an' cooin', jes' billin' an' cooin'—

IVORSEN. You're sure, now?

JEREMY. What do you want her to do, lay an egg?

IVORSEN. (*Laughs.*) Say, that's very *good—very* good! (*Heads for bathroom, pauses at door.*) Oh, when you get down to the office, tell them I'll be a little late. I want to go home and change. And you might tell them about my little announcement regarding your future with the firm.

JEREMY. Sir, you never *made* your little announcement!

IVORSEN. I didn't? . . . That's right, I didn't. Well, I'll tell you all about it at breakfast.

(*Exits into bathroom;* TINA *renews her unkinking efforts.*)

TINA. How does it feel, so far?

(CHARLIE *enters, sees them, starts downstairs with her clothes.*)

JEREMY. So far, so good.
CHARLIE. Shall I get my gypsy violin?
TINA. I am merely trying to repair Jeremy's spine.
CHARLIE. (*Crosses toward her, extending clothing.*) I suggest you put these on before trying anything strenuous —or would you rather I simply turned my back?
TINA. Well—maybe you're right. (*Releases* JEREMY, *who immediately rocks forward and cracks his head on the coffee table; she rushes around sofa, rocks him up, on:*) Oh, Jeremy, I'm so sorry! . . . Did you hurt your head?
JEREMY. That's all right, Tina. It took my mind off my back for a second.
CHARLIE. Here. You go put these things on. *I'll* attend to Jeremy—
JEREMY. Tina, don't you do it—
CHARLIE. (*Already half-dragging hapless* JEREMY *to Center of room.*) This . . . is going to . . . take more strength . . . than Tina can provide.
JEREMY. Then I'd just as soon stay like this. It's not so bad. It just takes getting used to.
CHARLIE. (*Brutally getting full nelson on him.*) Don't be a sissy—
TINA. (*Hovering in Right archway.*) You won't hurt him, Charlie?
CHARLIE. Only insofar as is absolutely necessary to the treatment!
TINA. Then I'll go see about some coffee. (*Exits with clothing into kitchen.*)
JEREMY. Charlie? Listen, Charlie, before you do anything, I'd like to explain to you about last night—

CHARLIE. (*Scrunching him erect on stressed words:*) But, Jeremy, old friend, *I* understood *per*-fect-ly—

JEREMY. (*Erect, but statue-stiff.*) Then—why did you get so mad?

CHARLIE. (*Thumping edge of hand experimentally along* JEREMY'S *front.*) Why, Jeremy! Whatever makes you think I'm . . . *mad?*

(*On last word, finds spot, judo-chops* JEREMY'S *solar plexus;* JEREMY *staggers back with a yell, then realizes he's unkinked.*)

KATHRYN. (*Bursts out of guestroom, dressed, on yell, concerned.*) Charlie! What did you do to Jeremy?

JEREMY. It's nothing, darling—I'm perfectly all right.

KATHRYN. (*Ices over, instantly.*) *Pity!* (*During next dialogue, holding herself coolly aloof, she descends, gets morning paper from front porch, crosses down to sofa, sits, and begins reading, as if deeply engrossed in what she's reading.*)

JEREMY. Well—anyhow—Charlie, thanks for fixing me up. I feel great!

CHARLIE. Enjoy your moment. I just didn't want to hit a helpless cripple—

JEREMY. Now hold on, Charlie! At least listen to my story—

CHARLIE. You mean we haven't heard *all* your stories? You really ought to put out an anthology.

(*Squares off to throw a punch, but* TINA *enters, dressed, carrying rolled-up sheet, gets between them.*)

TINA. Here, Jeremy, where do you want this stuff?

CHARLIE. Right there, behind him. It'll help break his fall—

TINA. Oh, stop acting like a caveman, Charlie. You have no reason to lose your temper—

CHARLIE. After last night?

TINA. Since when is what I do any business of yours, Charlie? Or may I call you "Mister Bickle"?

CHARLIE. Didn't last night—when you and I were on the sofa—didn't that mean anything to you at all?

TINA. (*Hopefully.*) Did it mean anything to *you?*

CHARLIE. (*Obviously, it did, but:*) Of course not!

TINA. Then what do *you* care *how* I spend my evenings? (*As he wobbles, stymied by this thrust, she turns to* JEREMY:) Where do you want these things, huh?

JEREMY. Oh. Sorry. Here, I'll take them. (*Carries them to window seat, stashes them inside it.*)

TINA. I'll go see how the coffee's doing.

(*She exits to kitchen;* CHARLIE *half-follows her, then stops, brooding, facing Upstage through Right Archway;* JEREMY *comes around to Left end of sofa, looks pleadingly at* KATHRYN, *who is still determinedly engrossed in the newspaper.*)

JEREMY. I don't suppose it would do the least bit of good to try and explain to you about last night?

KATHRYN. (*Eyes still on paper, turning page.*) The whole thing was a mistake? You're simply a victim of unfortunate circumstances?

JEREMY. That's it. That's precisely it.

KATHRYN. Hmmph! What *else* would a guilty man say?

JEREMY. Kathy, what else would an *innocent* man say?

(CHARLIE *sees yet-unseen* TINA *approaching, turns and hastily comes down to sofa, sits, takes part of paper, pretends to read, as:*)

TINA. (*Enters.*) The coffee's ready, but the toast will take a little longer.

KATHRYN. Why not just hold the bread between your hot little hands?

TINA. (*Stung, says sweetly through clenched teeth:*) Why not just stick it under your collar?

(*Both* WOMEN *start to move, ready to go at each other.*)

JEREMY. Now, *hold it*—everybody calm down! Kathryn, you and Charlie are just making *yourselves* miserable. If you'd sit still and *listen* to me for five minutes—

KATHRYN. Give me one good reason we should believe anything *you* tell us—

JEREMY. (*Earnestly, from the heart:*) Have I ever *lied* to you?

CHARLIE. (*As he and* KATHRYN *react simultaneously.*) *Wow!*

JEREMY. Damn it, you know what I mean. Will you just listen, please?

CHARLIE. (*As he and* KATHRYN *set down papers on coffee table, fold arms.*) Okay. Five minutes.

KATHRYN. This ought to be good—

JEREMY. It will be irrefutably good. (*Unconsciously plays scene like lawyer dealing with hostile witness.*) Now, the basic problem, as I see it, is that you two have assumed there is something romantic going on between myself and Tina. Is that correct?

CHARLIE. Those are not the precise terms I would have used—but—yes, in essence you are quite correct.

JEREMY. Very well. Now—when did this idea first occur to you?

KATHRYN. (*Exchanges a look with* CHARLIE, *then, as* TINA *and* JEREMY *smolder in exquisite silence,* KATHRYN *and* CHARLIE *do an impromptu and facetious "duet" until* JEREMY's *interruptive line.*) Oh, *let* me try to *recall* . . . Yes, I remember quite clearly, now: We were out on the balcony—

CHARLIE. Up there—

KATHRYN. Looking down into the living room—

CHARLIE. Down here—

KATHRYN. When we noticed that you—

CHARLIE. In a state approximating undress—

KATHRYN. —were in the vicinity of Miss Tina Winslow—

CHARLIE. In a state approximating the Venus de Milo—

KATHRYN. And I distinctly remember remarking to myself, "Why—there seems to be something *romantic* going on between them!"

(*She and* CHARLIE *resume reading newspaper on:*)

CHARLIE. *That* answer your question, bub?

JEREMY. Perfectly! So—you noticed all this from the balcony, did you? And what were you *doing* on that balcony?

CHARLIE. Getting an eyeful!

JEREMY. I mean, what brought you out onto the balcony in the first place!?

TINA. (*Catches his drift, blurts helpfully:*) I screamed.

JEREMY. (*Faces Downstage, folding arms triumphantly, for:*) Exactly! And *who's* ever heard of a young lady *screaming* when she's having a *good* time with a *man?* (*In unison,* CHARLIE *and* KATHRYN *slam down their papers onto the coffee table, faces icy with insult, and circle their respective ends of the sofa and march stiffly out into the kitchen, as* JEREMY—*his face slowly showing a realization of the dopey "trump card" he has played— stands right where he is, his own face a study in dawning horror; he turns Upstage just before the* Two *of them vanish into kitchen, and cries with poignant hindsight:*) I WITHDRAW THE QUESTION!

TINA. It's no use, Jeremy! They've decided what's what, and there's no changing their minds for them.

JEREMY. (*Slumped, defeated.*) I should have my head examined for even trying. Why would anyone believe *me,* Jeremy Troy, any more? I've been so busy being clever all my life that I never took the trouble to bother with simple honesty. Now I'm getting just what I deserve— what *any* liar deserves!

TINA. (*Softly.*) You're crazy about her, aren't you!

JEREMY. I didn't think it showed, this morning.

TINA. Oh, Jeremy, you can't stop fighting, not now—

JEREMY. Well—I'll keep up appearances till Ivorsen leaves, anyhow—

IVORSEN. (*Enters from bathroom.*) Kathryn—I'm afraid I won't have time to join you for breakfast.

TINA. I'll manage.

IVORSEN. Splendid, splendid! (*Exits into bedroom.*)

JEREMY. Excuse me, I have to get ready for work!

(*Starts upstairs as* KATHRYN *and* CHARLIE, *with tray of coffee, toast, etc., enter from kitchen;* TINA *sees them, starts for upper Left archway as he exits into bedroom.*)

TINA. And I have a long walk to modeling school!

KATHRYN. Tina, you're not going *now*—?

TINA. (*Whirls just below archway.*) You just watch me!

CHARLIE. (*Leaving coffee, etc., on coffee table, starts toward her.*) But—you've got to be here when Ivorsen comes down—

TINA. (*A mocking reversion to southern drawl, for:*) No, thank you! (*Gets coat, purse, from behind fireplace, as:*)

CHARLIE. Tina, this might cost Jeremy his job . . . He'd lose everything—the north light—the guest room—the *guest*—

TINA. (*In archway, donning coat.*) I don't think Jeremy much cares, any more.

KATHRYN. But I can't have him throwing away seven years hard work, no matter what's happened—

TINA. (*This is too much; she plunks purse down on desk, turns to face them, arms akimbo; throughout her speech, while they sense the semantic drift of it, their faces slowly react to the wording:*) What about his seven years' work on *you*? *Those* were hard, *too!* What do you think it *means* to him to have things he wanted take over things he didn't want—even if he pretended he did? You can't let him *do* it. Not when he doesn't *care* if he does or not—unless *you* do. If you knew how he felt—how he *still* feels—or—how maybe he *doesn't* feel any more—but still *wants* to—you'd be the first one to *tell* him so! But *do* you? *Do* you? No! . . . Because . . . because . . . Oh—*don't* you *know* what you're *doing?* (*Turns, nearly in tears, grabs purse.*)

KATHRYN. (*Sensing the truth, but mystified by foregoing explanation of it.*) Tina—when we came out on the balcony last night—?

TINA. (*Whirls to face her, furious.*) The only thing that happened last night was one large scream from me because Jeremy sat on my stomach! It's your own fault for locking your bedroom door—I knocked, you know!

KATHRYN. That was *you* at my door? And when you couldn't get in . . .

TINA. I thought the sofa had been laid out for me, and took it. My mistake, and I'm sorry! (*Turns, starts toward front door.*)

KATHRYN. (*Slowly moving toward sofa, almost speaking to herself:*) No. *My* mistake. And *I'm* sorry . . .

TINA. Jeremy needs an apology worse than I do.

CHARLIE. Tina, wait! (*But when she turns, eagerly, he loses his nerve, and hedges:*) I—I haven't captured your kneecaps yet.

TINA. Then I'll *mail* you a *picture!* (*Half-turns, remembers something, takes piece of paper from purse, turns back and hands it to him, elaborately casual.*) Oh, and you'd better have this. I made it out in the kitchen.

CHARLIE. What's this?

TINA. A check to pay for Mister Ivorsen's car, of course. Don't say I never did anything for you. So long, Charlie Bickle . . . It's been—a real experience! (*Her voice breaks on last word; she exits hurriedly out front door.*)

CHARLIE. (*Reads aloud from check:*) "Seventeen thousand dollars"! (*To* KATHRYN, *now seated glumly on sofa.*) Who does she think she is? (*Reads on, and an-*

swers own question:) "Tina Winslow *Roc-ke-fel-ler—?*"
(*Gallops out after* TINA, *waving check like a madman.*)
TIN.\AAAAAAA!

(*We hear front DOOR slam; at same moment,* IVORSEN
—*now dapper in his tux again*—*enters from bedroom, closes door, sees to his delight that "the
princess" is alone, hastens downstairs;* KATHRYN,
meanwhile, after rolling her eyes grimly during
CHARLIE'S *exit, has taken a piece of dry toast and is
stolidly ripping it apart with her teeth, bite by grim
bite; at foot of stairs,* IVORSEN *clicks his heels and
bows; she looks his way, narrow-eyed.*)

IVORSEN. Your Highness! (*Crosses to her blithely, on:*)
I must say you are looking absolutely radiant this morning! (*She isn't, and she knows it, and she returns to a
down-front introspective stare, tearing monotonously at
her toast.*) Mere words cannot express the thrill I feel at
knowing a genuine princess! . . . May I sit beside you?
(*Without looking up, she hitches over, munching still; he
sits.*) You know, Your Highness, I was very impressed
last night with the way you answered the telephone . . .
Why, you even helped clear away the plates! It set me
wondering—do you think it might be possible—so that I
have a memory to carry away with me—that you might
. . . butter me a piece of toast? (*He waits, hoping on
hope;* KATHRYN *slowly turns, looks at this fluttering,
unctuous ninny; then, she smiles; it is a strange smile;
setting down her own toast, she proceeds to lavish a fresh
piece with butter, spreading it thicker and thicker and
with increasing personal relish, as he babbles onward.*)
Oh, thank you, Your Highness! As the years go by, I will
always treasure this moment. And when I am feeling blue,
amid the cares of my workaday world, I will ever be able
to find happiness by simply recalling the morning the
Princess of Rumania buttered my morning toast, and—
(*His hand has been outstretched, palm upward;* KATHRYN

slaps the toast onto it, butter-side down, daintily wipes her fingertips on a napkin, leans back nonchalantly and folds her arms; he stares at the toast for a long moment; then speaks quietly:) Why did you do that?

KATHRYN. (*Rises, moves to Right end of sofa, faces him over its arm.*) Because *I* am Kathryn Troy— (*Sweeping gesture at room.*) this is *my* house— (*A snarl.*) and I'll do anything I damn please in it! (*Starts toward kitchen, stops, turns back, snaps:*) Put *that* in your brief and plead it! (*Exits triumphantly into kitchen.*)

IVORSEN. (*Turns back from looking at her, looks at toast, then out front.*) Who was that lady I saw him with *last* night? (*Stands, starts for kitchen.*) Ingeborg? . . . Mrs. Troy? . . . I'm coming out, *whoever* you are! (*Exits into kitchen on:*) Would you mind telling me what this is all about?

KATHRYN. (*Off, loud:*) I'D *LOVE* TO!

(JEREMY *enters from bedroom in fresh suit, etc., comes downstairs, steps into Left archway, gets overcoat from behind fireplace, comes down to coffee table donning overcoat, lifts piece of toast, tries to butter it, finds butter dish empty, sets down knife with an I-might-have-*known *grunt, takes dry toast to window, stands munching it, looking out, resignedly and wearily;* KATHRYN, *then* IVORSEN, *enter from kitchen, cross to Downstage Left, not seeing* JEREMY *at window, on:*)

IVORSEN. Kathryn, I can hardly believe it! Do you mean to tell me that— (JEREMY, *hearing them, starts toward them, gets almost to* IVORSEN'S *back as he realizes what is being said, panics, rushes back to try and hide in window seat, but it's too small, compromises by yanking drapes shut before him as he stands in open window seat, his piece of dry toast protruding, trembling, at overlap, during:*) all these years Jeremy has had no degree—?

Has never, in fact, even attended law school? And then, last night, passed off another woman as his wife, his wife as a comparative stranger, and an old friend as his own wife's fiance—and fooled *me?*

KATHRYN. Yes, sir, that's exactly what happened.

IVORSEN. (*Turns Upstage, bellows toward bedroom.*) *JEREMY!* (*The drapes swish back: he and* KATHRYN *turn to look, see* JEREMY.)

JEREMY. Here, sir! (*Steps from window seat, crosses to* IVORSEN, *stops, says bravely:*) Guilty as charged!

IVORSEN. (*Ominously.*) When I meet a man who is living a lie . . . a man who cons other people into living even bigger lies . . . a man whose entire life has been founded on deceit, double-dealing and duplicity—there is only one conclusion to be reached: There stands a real— *lawyer!* . . . (*He grins broadly on final word, extends his Upstage hand, and* JEREMY—*briefly frozen in unbelief —grasps it dazedly, and thereby getting the dry side of the buttered toast, on:*) *Partner!*

JEREMY. (*Echoes, stunned:*) "Partner"? Sir, I— (*Looks in confusion from own toast to new piece in other hand.*) I don't know what to say—

IVORSEN. You might say "Thank you" to your wife. She's the one who told me all about it.

JEREMY. (*Goes toward her, arms outstretched.*) Kathy—!

KATHRYN. (*As they embrace awkwardly, his toast-filled hands extended out behind her.*) Darling!

IVORSEN. Listen, I've got to dash off for New York, but before I go I want to make that announcement I forgot to make last night at dinner.

KATHRYN. But—wasn't that the partnership?

IVORSEN. Of course not. Until today, I had no idea what great lawyer material Jeremy was. I was just going to tell him that since he did such a great job on that legal brief I was going to let him plead the case in court!

JEREMY. But sir—I've never taken the bar exam.

IVORSEN. You have your choice of taking it in Manhattan, Albany or Buffalo.

JEREMY. Well, sir—that's a two-day exam . . . I'll need a little time to prepare for it—-

IVORSEN. Then consider yourself on a paid vacation, starting right now, until after the exam.

CHARLIE. (*Bursts in through front door, towing* TINA *by the hand, down to* GROUP.) Hey, everybody, we're getting married!

TINA. (*Belatedly reacts to* IVORSEN's *presence, goes into drawl:*) Why, Charlie, what would Mister Ivorsen think! You *know* I'll never leave Jeremy!

(*Then she and* CHARLIE *do a bewildered take, as:*)

IVORSEN. (*Matter-of-factly waves down her disclaimer:*) Aw, go ahead!

JEREMY. Kathy— How about Buffalo? It's not far from Niagara Falls, and we never did have a real honeymoon—

KATHRYN. But—Jeremy, how can you take the exam? You have no degree!

IVORSEN. In New York State he doesn't need it. Four years' clerking in a law office is sufficient. You've had *seven*—partner! (*Goes up behind fireplace.*)

CHARLIE. (*Crosses Left with* TINA, *she continues on to* KATHRYN, *as he stops.*) Partner? Jeremy-boy, can an apologetic old buddy congratulate you? (*They shake hands,* CHARLIE *gets the butter-side of the toast; he stares at it, then goes to coffee table for napkin to wipe it, on:*)

KATHRYN. (*Woman-to-woman.*) Tina, wait'll my friends find out you're a Rockefeller!

TINA. (*Looks to see that* CHARLIE's *out of earshot, as* JEREMY *leans in closer, fascinated by what* KATHRYN *said; then:*) Wait'll the *Rockefellers* find out!

(*As* KATHRYN *and* JEREMY *turn delighted gazes at* CHARLIE's *back,* TINA *lackadaisically buffs her nails on the lapel of her coat; then* IVORSEN *comes from behind fireplace, down between* CHARLIE *and others.*)

IVORSEN. I can't find my overcoat—
CHARLIE. (*Turns, says amicably:*) Never mind your *overcoat*—don't miss your *bus!*

(TINA *reacts with laughter,* IVORSEN *staring, at sea.*)

JEREMY. Omigosh! Mister Ivorsen, I just remembered one more requirement for taking that exam: I have to have at least six months' residency in New York State—
IVORSEN. Good heavens, you're right! I don't know *how* we're going to get around *this* one . . .

(*As he says this, here is the position of players:* CHARLIE *is Downstage Right, just above the coffee table,* IVORSEN *is Downstage Center, and* JEREMY, KATHRYN *and* TINA *are Downstage Left;* ALL *stay perfectly still for one beat; then they begin to pace, thinking hard:* CHARLIE *crosses to Downstage Left,* IVORSEN *to downstage Right,* TINA *to Upstage Left archway,* KATHRYN *to Upstage Right archway, and* JEREMY *to* CHARLIE'S *former position just above the coffee table; on* CHARLIE'S *line,* ALL *turn to face him.*)

CHARLIE. I've got it! (*Crosses to* JEREMY *on:*) I have to get a new apartment in the Village. Why don't I take out the lease under your name?
TINA. (*Comes Downstage left on:*) And you could advance us six months' back rent—
KATHRYN. (*To* TINA, *coming down to Center Stage, facing her.*) You could use it to bribe the landlord to say that Jeremy had lived there all that time—
JEREMY. (*Crosses directly to* TINA *on:*) And *you* could move in under *Kathryn's* name—
IVORSEN. (*Comes up to stand Right of* KATHRYN *on:*) And *I* could swear I'd visited Jeremy there *lots* of times—
TINA. (*Crosses to* CHARLIE *on:*) I can probably talk my father into calling me "Kathryn" whenever he visits—

CHARLIE. Why not tell him *my* name's *Jeremy?* We've never met!

JEREMY. We'll buy you magazine subscriptions under *my* name—

KATHRYN. (*Goes to him, embraces him, on:*) Oh, Jeremy—I'm *so* glad I finally told the *truth!*

(PLAYERS *are now ranged, from Right:* CHARLIE *and* TINA, IVORSEN, *and* JEREMY *and* KATHRYN; *as* CHARLIE *and* TINA *embrace:*)

IVORSEN. (*Out front:*) Well—it's like I've always maintained: Honesty is the best policy!

(*And the PORTRAIT of George Washington falls with a crash to the balcony;* ALL *react, startled, turn to ascertain source of the sound, and the* FIVESOME, *backs to us, are staring upward, as:*)

THE CURTAIN FALLS

PROPERTY PLOT

ACT ONE

Preset:
  Empty tumbler on mantel
  Strongbox (containing graduation photo, diploma, assorted papers) in deep drawer of desk
  Legal brief on desk
  Phonebook (yellow pages) on desk
  Elephant statuette on desk

Carried On:

  Kathryn:
    Ice cube tray, cufflinks in it
    Tray with filled coffeepot, 2 cups, plate of donuts
    Broken Coffeemate jar-bottom

  Jeremy:
    Briefcase
    Pills in small bottle
    Wallet with money in it

  Charlie:
    Duffel bag, easel, paintbox, painting, brushes
    Tray of ice cubes
    Full cup of coffee

  Tina:
    Large handbag containing slippers, handmirror and comb

ACT TWO

Preset:
  Phonebook open on desk
  Graduation photo and diploma in frames over mantel
  Blanket, sheet, pillow and pillowcase in window seat

Carried On:

  Ivorsen:
    Car keys on chain in overcoat pocket
    Single place setting

96

CHARLIE:
Small tray with 2 martinis
Small tray of hors d'oeuvres
Single martini

JEREMY:
One martini

TINA:
Rolling table set for 4, with bottle of wine on it
Soup tureen, with soup and ladle
Dinner gong and striker
Large tray with platter of "chicken in the wood," tongs, 4
empty plates and single plate with ham sandwich
Tray with pre-sliced pie on individual plates, forks
Towel to hand to Charlie

ACT THREE

PRESET: (*none*)

CARRIED ON:

KATHRYN:
Tray with coffeepot, cups, plate of toast, dish of butter,
butter knife
Newspaper

TINA:
Check to give Charlie in her purse

CHARLIE:
Sketchpad and pencil
Tina's clothes

"HERE LIES JEREMY TROY"
STAGE PLAN

UPPER LEVEL

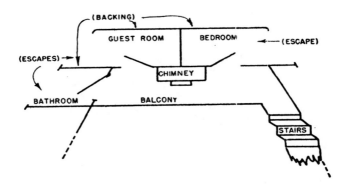

LOWER LEVEL

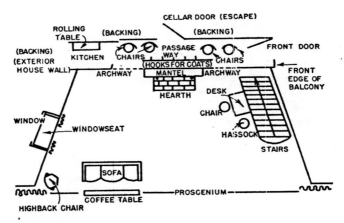

SKIN DEEP
Jon Lonoff

Comedy / 2m, 2f / Interior Unit Set

In *Skin Deep*, a large, lovable, lonely-heart, named Maureen Mulligan, gives romance one last shot on a blind-date with sweet awkward Joseph Spinelli; she's learned to pepper her speech with jokes to hide insecurities about her weight and appearance, while he's almost dangerously forthright, saying everything that comes to his mind. They both know they're perfect for each other, and in time they come to admit it.

They were set up on the date by Maureen's sister Sheila and her husband Squire, who are having problems of their own: Sheila undergoes a non-stop series of cosmetic surgeries to hang onto the attractive and much-desired Squire, who may or may not have long ago held designs on Maureen, who introduced him to Sheila. With Maureen particularly vulnerable to both hurting and being hurt, the time is ripe for all these unspoken issues to bubble to the surface.

"Warm-hearted comedy ... the laughter was literally show-stopping. A winning play, with enough good-humored laughs and sentiment to keep you smiling from beginning to end."
- TalkinBroadway.com

"It's a little Paddy Chayefsky, a lot Neil Simon and a quick-witted, intelligent voyage into the not-so-tranquil seas of middle-aged love and dating. The dialogue is crackling and hilarious; the plot simple but well-turned; the characters endearing and quirky; and lurking beneath the merriment is so much heartache that you'll stand up and cheer when the unlikely couple makes it to the inevitable final clinch."
- NYTheatreWorld.Com

COCKEYED
William Missouri Downs

Comedy / 3m, 1f / Unit Set

Phil, an average nice guy, is madly in love with the beautiful Sophia. The only problem is that she's unaware of his existence. He tries to introduce himself but she looks right through him. When Phil discovers Sophia has a glass eye, he thinks that might be the problem, but soon realizes that she really can't see him. Perhaps he is caught in a philosophical hyperspace or dualistic reality or perhaps beautiful women are just unaware of nice guys. Armed only with a B.A. in philosophy, Phil sets out to prove his existence and win Sophia's heart. This fast moving farce is the winner of the HotCity Theatre's GreenHouse New Play Festival. The St. Louis Post-Dispatch called Cockeyed a clever romantic comedy, Talkin' Broadway called it "hilarious," while Playback Magazine said that it was "fresh and invigorating."

Winner!
of the HotCity Theatre GreenHouse New Play Festival

"Rocking with laughter...hilarious...polished and engaging work draws heavily on the age-old conventions of farce: improbable situations, exaggerated characters, amazing coincidences, absurd misunderstandings, people hiding in closets and barely missing each other as they run in and out of doors...full of comic momentum as Cockeyed hurtles toward its conclusion."
- Talkin' Broadway

LaVergne, TN USA
27 January 2011
214227LV00007B/42/P